The Amish Suitor

Jo Ann Brown

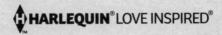 HARLEQUIN® LOVE INSPIRED®

Recycling programs
for this product may
not exist in your area.

LOVE INSPIRED BOOKS

ISBN-13: 978-1-335-50952-9

The Amish Suitor

Copyright © 2018 by Jo Ann Ferguson

www.Harlequin.com

Printed in U.S.A.

"The more we work together, the quicker you will learn.

Kyle must learn to face you and enunciate when he speaks."

"Enough what when he speaks?"

"E-nun-ci-ate. To say something clearly."

Eli nodded, flustered he'd misunderstood Miriam.

She touched his face. Startled, he froze.

"Eli, do not be embarrassed. Even people with perfect hearing miss words."

Was his pain emblazoned there? The last thing he wanted was her pity.

He realized how he'd misread her when she said, "Your hearing loss is nothing to be ashamed of."

"I know."

"You say that. But you do not act that way. It will get easier." She smiled as if he were one of her scholars.

Was that how she saw him? That *was* what he was, but when she touched him on his arm to get his attention, he couldn't think of her as anything other than a charming woman.

She was his teacher—and his neighbor. Nothing else. He was being a fool. He wasn't going to invite more pain into his life. Not when he'd come to Harmony Creek to start over.

Jo Ann Brown has always loved stories with happily-ever-after endings. A former military officer, she is thrilled to have the chance to write stories about people falling in love. She is also a photographer and travels with her husband of more than thirty years to places where she can snap pictures. They have three children and live in Florida. Drop her a note at joannbrownbooks.com.

Books by Jo Ann Brown

Love Inspired

Amish Spinster Club

The Amish Suitor

Amish Hearts

Amish Homecoming
An Amish Match
His Amish Sweetheart
An Amish Reunion
A Ready-Made Amish Family
An Amish Proposal
An Amish Arrangement

Be strong and of a good courage,
fear not, nor be afraid of them:
for the Lord thy God, he it is that doth go with thee;
he will not fail thee, nor forsake thee.
—*Deuteronomy* 31:6

For Gary Rubin
the "younger man"
A dear friend for longer than either of us
wants to admit!
Do you still remember the parade in Hop Bottom
with one marching band and nineteen fire engines?

Chapter One

Harmony Creek Hollow, New York

The bottle of spaghetti sauce at the top of the pyramid swayed.

The three bottles below it rocked.

The whole stack quivered.

Eli Troyer leaped forward and hooked an arm around his nephew. He yanked the six-year-old away from the grocery store endcap. Kyle let out a shriek. Whether it was shock or a forewarning, everyone within sight in the small grocery store froze.

But not the bottles. The stack began to crumble.

Just as the wall had.

Irrational terror swelled through Eli, clamping talons around his windpipe. He couldn't breathe. He couldn't move. Sounds erupted in his mind. The memory of an earsplitting crack from a wall that couldn't stand any longer. A man's horrified shout, a woman's scream, crashing stone, pain…silence.

Always the silence.

Knowing he had to protect the little boy, Eli put out

a hand in a futile effort to stabilize the bottles, to keep the display from crumbling. Too late. Just like before. In a slow-motion avalanche, the tower collapsed. He bent over Kyle, keeping himself between the little boy and disaster. Time escalated again when the first jar hit the concrete floor and shattered. The rest followed. Some bounced and rolled, but most exploded in a spray of marinara sauce. The sharp sounds resonated through his hearing aids as if he stood in a giant hailstorm.

Shouts, loud enough so he could hear them, though he couldn't pick out words, rang through the store. His fear faded into knowing he must deal with what had happened in Salem's only grocery store. He fought the yearning to flee as a different panic burst out in a cold sweat. After four years of staying out of the lime- light, eyes were focused on him. It was the moment he dreaded, the moment he'd hoped wouldn't come.

Someone was going to talk to him. Ask him questions. Expect him to understand what they'd said and then answer.

What once would have been a snap now was tor- ture. Since the retaining wall had fallen on him and his brother and sister-in-law, he'd asked God at least once a day why Kyle's parents had been killed and he hadn't. He'd survived, but most of his hearing had been lost, leaving him encased in silence.

Not just his hearing had changed that day. His whole life had. If the wall hadn't capsized, he'd be married to Betty Ann Miller. He hadn't been sure if her averted glances had been pity or if she was ashamed because she found herself walking out with a damaged man. Ei- ther way, he never walked out with her again, and she'd married someone else.

He avoided talking to people. Most when they saw

his hearing aids raised their voices and spoke slowly as if that would have helped more. Before he'd brought Kyle north from their home district in Delaware, he'd known when to dodge chatty neighbors. The storekeepers near Dover had learned it was easier to let him point to what he needed and not engage him in conversation.

Ach, how he missed the simple pleasure of a chat. Now he mostly spoke to Kyle, who helped him with even the simplest interactions.

"Are you okay?" he asked his nephew.

The little boy, who looked like Eli's late brother with his bright red hair and freckles, nodded.

"What happened?"

Kyle shrugged and held up a box of brown sugar before going to stand by where the sugar was on a shelf. It was at least three feet from the endcap, farther than the little boy could reach. The motions were Kyle's way of telling him that he hadn't touched the bottles.

His mud-brown eyes widened, and he pointed past Eli.

Expecting to see an angry store manager, Eli squared his shoulders and prepared to strain what little hearing he had left to pick up the manager's words. He turned.

And stared.

On the other side of the broken bottles and splattered sauce stood two women and two half-filled shopping carts. An elderly *Englisch* woman cowered behind her cart and peered like a cartoon owl through glasses with bright green frames. The other woman stood in front of her.

Eli's breath caught as he looked at the pretty Amish woman. He hadn't attended a church service in Harmony Creek Hollow yet, because he and Kyle had just moved into the new settlement earlier in the week. But he guessed she was the sister of the settlement's founder, Caleb Hartz, because beneath her heart-shaped *kapp*, she had similar pale blond hair and intense jade green eyes. As well, she had her brother's impressive height.

Her apron and the hem of her dark purple dress, as well as her black sneakers, had been showered with spaghetti sauce. A dab highlighted her left cheekbone. Pink was returning to her cheeks, replacing the gray of shock.

Kyle grasped his hand tightly. They stood side by side when a harried *Englischer* wearing a bright red bib apron as the cashiers did rushed to him. The man, whom Eli surmised was the store manager because he wore a white shirt and tie, pushed past the crowd of shoppers toward the elderly *Englisch* woman.

"Okay...boy?" he asked, stopping to look at Eli.

Before Eli could answer, the elderly woman waved her hands, gesturing toward him and Kyle. He struggled to follow the conversation as Kyle's grip grew more constricting.

Guessing the old woman was accusing Kyle of causing the sauce bottles to fall, Eli said, "See here—"

The tall Amish woman—Eli thought Caleb had said his sister's name was Miriam—turned to help the older woman stand straighter. The *Englisch* woman was getting more upset, and Miriam bent to speak with her.

He opened his mouth, but Kyle tugged on his sleeve. When he looked at the little boy, his nephew shook his head. Did Kyle want him to say nothing?

Straining his ears, he tried to hear what was going on and why Miriam Hartz was getting involved.

"The boy didn't do anything." Miriam saw the shock on the faces of the three friends she'd come with to the

Salem Market, but she wasn't going to watch in silence while a *kind* was falsely accused.

She guessed the little boy was Kyle Troyer, because she'd met the other *kinder* who lived along Harmony Creek. After the little boy and his *onkel* had arrived from Delaware, Caleb had gone to their house at the far end of the hollow, but she hadn't joined him. She'd sent a chicken-and-noodles casserole as well as vegetable soup and a few jars of the grape jelly she'd brought from Lancaster County. Caleb had said Eli wasn't talkative, but seemed determined to make a home for himself and his nephew.

She realized her brother had left out a few details. Details like how tall Eli was. She wasn't accustomed to looking up to meet anyone's eyes other than Caleb's, but when the newcomer's gaze caught hers, the startlingly blue eyes beneath his dark brown hair that was in need of a trim were a half foot above hers. Next to his left eye, a small crescent scar matched another on his chin. Neither detracted from his *gut* looks.

"You're wrong!" The angry woman's piercing voice broke Miriam's mesmerism with the stranger. She pointed a gnarled finger toward the scared little boy. "He's the one who did it!"

"Are you certain, Mrs. Hayes?" asked the dark-haired man who stood beside the woman. A name tag pinned on the red apron's bib showed he was the manager and his name was Russ. "You may not have seen clearly. You're wearing your reading glasses."

"I know what I saw!" Mrs. Hayes ripped off her glasses and let them drop on a chain hanging around her neck and set another, more sedate, pair on her nose.

The manager hesitated, and Miriam thought he was going to listen to the old woman.

Every instinct told her to remain silent, but she couldn't. She wondered why Eli Troyer wasn't defending his nephew. The *kind* reminded her of Ralph Fisher, the little boy whom she'd thought would become her son. The two boys were close in age. Seeing the *kind* sent a wave of regret through her. She'd lost everything the day Ralph almost drowned. His *daed*, Yost, had put an end to their marriage plans, telling her the near tragedy was her fault.

She hadn't thought so because the little boy hadn't been in her care when he got into trouble. True, he'd been on his way to her house where she was going to watch him that afternoon, but she hadn't expected him to arrive until much later. Shouts for help from his friends had reached her, and she'd pulled the little boy from the pond and got him breathing by the time the ambulance arrived. The little boy had survived and was fine, though he'd had a lesson about showing off she hoped he wouldn't forget.

She hadn't expected praise for doing what anyone would have done. Nor had she expected Yost's anger and the repercussions and recriminations that followed. However, as time went on and others seemed to believe her ex-fiancé, she'd started doubting herself. No one else could blame her more than she did herself. She'd been a teacher for more than eight years and knew what trouble a six-year-old boy could find. Though she'd glanced out the window to watch for Ralph, she hadn't gone to meet him. Her prayers that God would show her if the mistake was really hers hadn't been answered, so she'd stayed away from *kinder*. In case Yost was right.

Her arms ached to hold the frightened little boy next to Eli and offer him comfort. But she couldn't let herself be responsible for another *kind*. Next time it might not be an almost-tragedy.

Still, she couldn't stand there and let a young boy be accused wrongly.

Those thoughts fled through her mind in a second. Stepping forward, she said with a gentle smile, "Ma'am, I think there's been a misunderstanding."

The manager glanced at her with relief. He was ready for someone else to try to reason with Mrs. Hayes.

The old woman wasn't in a reasonable mood. "That boy bumped me a few minutes ago and almost knocked me off my feet. I'm sure he did the same to the sauce."

"Did you see him do that?" asked a voice from the crowd of onlookers.

Mrs. Hayes glowered. "I didn't have to. He was running wild. That man—" She aimed her frown at Eli. "I don't know how you people raise your kids, but they need to learn manners."

"I didn't mean to bump her," the little boy said. "She stopped right in front of me. It was an accident."

"Wouldn't have mattered if I'd fallen and broken a hip, would it, boy?"

"Let's be thankful that didn't happen," Miriam said. "Why don't you let him help you load your groceries into your car? That way, he'll have another chance to say he's sorry."

The *kind* glanced at his *onkel* and made motions with his hands.

Looking from him to her, Eli nodded.

"I can help you," the little boy said, sticking out his narrow chest.

The elderly woman seemed to have second thoughts as if she'd just realized how young the *kind* was. "No, that's not necessary." She frowned at Eli again. "You need to keep a closer watch on your child, and both of you need to learn how to behave in a store." With a muttered comment Miriam didn't catch, she walked away, pushing her cart.

The manager stepped forward, careful to skirt the broken glass. He motioned for a couple of his teen employees to start cleaning up the mess. He apologized to her and to Eli, ending with, "Mrs. Hayes means well."

"I understand," Miriam replied.

Eli said, *"Danki."*

His voice was a rich tenor as smooth as warm molasses. She wished he'd say more, but he didn't.

When Russ offered to pay to have her clothing cleaned, Miriam assured him it wasn't necessary. She wasn't sure she'd be able to get the stains out, but she didn't want to hand her clothes over to a stranger. The manager insisted on giving her a discount on her groceries, and she agreed after realizing she'd become the center of attention in the cramped store.

"You, too, sir," he said to Eli.

Again, Eli didn't reply until his nephew tugged on his arm. *"Danki."*

He took his nephew by the shoulders and steered him to a cart farther back in the aisle. When he glanced at her again, their gazes locked. Did he want to say something to her?

For the third time, he said, *"Danki."*

The single word's warmth and the sincerity in his voice swirled through her like a spring breeze after a difficult winter.

"You're welcome," she replied.

After he gave her a slight nod, he and his nephew walked away.

And Miriam let the air in her lungs sift out. She hadn't realized she'd been holding her breath, and she wasn't sure why she'd been.

"Are you okay, Miriam?" asked a soft voice from behind her.

As Eli and his nephew went around the end of the aisle and out of view, Miriam turned to her friend Annie Wagler. Annie, her twin sister, Leanna, and Sarah Kuhns had come with Miriam in the *Englisch* van they'd hired to bring them the three miles into Salem for grocery shopping. The other women were, like Miriam, in their midtwenties and unmarried. Each had come to the Harmony Creek settlement to join members of their families in making a new home. The twins lived with grandparents and their brother and his family while Sarah kept house for two brothers.

"I am. *Danki* for asking. I never expected so much excitement." She was babbling. She needed to stop, but her mouth kept moving. "Be careful. Glass is scattered everywhere."

"Bend down." Annie plucked a shard from the top of Miriam's *kapp*.

Annie was the complete opposite of Miriam. A tiny brunette doll instead of a female Goliath towering over everyone else as Miriam did. Annie possessed a sparkling effervescence that brightened every life she touched...which Miriam couldn't. Annie was honestly cheerful while Miriam had to struggle for every smile, though it'd been easier this morning while she and the other women rode in a white van driven by Hank Puente, who wasn't much taller than the Wagler twins.

While Annie handed the glass to a store employee, Miriam shook her apron and dress with care. She was shocked when several more pieces of glass dropped to the floor. When she washed her clothes and herself, she was going to have to take care not to get cut.

Sarah stepped forward. She was a couple inches taller than the twins, but had hair as red as Eli's nephew. She wore gold-rimmed glasses, which she pushed up on her freckled nose as she helped Annie and Leanna do a quick check to make sure there was no glass among the groceries in Miriam's cart. Other shoppers edged around them, staring. Not at the plain women, but at the mess. More than one *Englisch* woman asked if Miriam had gotten hurt.

Miriam was amazed how the incident had opened the door wider for them with their *Englisch* neighbors, who had watched the Amish newcomers with polite but distancing curiosity. When she mentioned that to her friends, Annie giggled.

"What's the saying? An ill wind blows no *gut*? I'd say it's the opposite today. *Gut* things are happening."

Annie saw the positive side of every situation, one of the reasons Miriam was glad they'd become friends. Annie's optimism helped counteract her own regrets at how her betrothal had ended.

As she moved her cart aside so the store employees could clean the floor, she saw Eli and his nephew checking out. She watched the little boy signal his *onkel* each time the cashier spoke to them. Comprehension blossomed when she remembered Caleb saying Eli wore two hearing aids. They must not be enough to compensate for Eli's hearing loss because he needed help from his nephew.

"Someone's curious about our newcomer," Leanna said.

"I'm more curious how long the checkout lines are," she replied.

With another giggle, Annie said, "She's not denying it."

Miriam shook her head and looked at Sarah, who was more serious than she was. They shrugged before separating to finish their shopping.

Ten minutes later Miriam was watching her purchases flow along the belt at the checkout. Coming into the small village to do errands had become more fun than she'd expected. Other than the spaghetti sauce disaster, but that would be amusing when she told her brother about it. She was glad she'd accepted the invitation to share a ride with the Wagler twins and Sarah Kuhns.

Hearing laughter, she grinned at Annie. The tiny woman was in a silly mood today. They were enjoying a respite from the hard work of making homes out of the rough buildings on the farms where they lived.

It hadn't taken long to get their groceries. The store had only three rows of shelves and was much smaller than the big-box store where Miriam used to shop at in Lancaster County. She hadn't gone with women friends then, but with Ralph.

Her happiness faded again at the thought of the little boy she'd believed was going to be her son when she married his *daed.*

"*Ach*, Miriam, where did you find those oyster crackers?" asked Annie.

"I think," she replied, "the crackers are in the middle aisle."

Telling her twin to stay with their cart, Annie sprinted away as if she were as young as the boy with Eli. Two men at the other register followed her with their eyes. Nobody could be unaware of the interest Annie Wagler drew from men, except Annie herself.

"That's forty-nine dollars and twenty-seven cents," the cashier said. In a singsongy tone that suggested she repeated the words many times each day, she asked, "Do you have one of our frequent shopper cards? You get a point for every dollar you spend. When you fill the card, you get twenty-five bucks off your next visit. If…" The woman paused. "Do you people use these sorts of cards?"

Miriam smiled at the woman whose hair was the same rich purple as Miriam's dress. After five months, *Englischers* around Salem still worried about offending the plain folks who'd moved into their midst.

"*Ja*… I mean, yes," Miriam said, wanting to put the other woman at ease. "We're known for being frugal."

"Squeezing a penny until it calls uncle, huh?" The cashier laughed as she pulled out a card and handed it to Miriam. "Bring this with you every time you shop."

"Thank you." She put the card in her wallet and pulled out cash to pay for her groceries. "Do you take checks here?"

"As long as they are local and have a phone number on them."

With another smile, Miriam accepted her change and helped the cashier bag her groceries. She put the grocery bags in her cart and walked toward the automatic door. As it swung open, she walked out. She watched a buggy leave the parking lot. It wasn't a gray buggy like the ones she was accustomed to, nor was it the shape of the black buggy Sarah's brothers had brought from northern Indiana. Though the departing buggy was also black, it was wider. It had to belong to the Troyers, because when she'd visited a cousin in Delaware, she'd seen similar Amish buggies.

Once their *Ordnung* was decided, everyone in the new settlement would drive identical buggies. Discussion had begun on the rules for their church district, but nothing had been voted on yet.

Hearing the store's door opening behind her, Miriam hurried toward the white van. Hank slid aside the door as she reached it. He reminded her of a squirrel with his quick motions and gray hair and beard. He wore a backward gold baseball cap as well as a purple and gold jacket, though the June day was warm. He'd explained the coat was to support the local high school team.

"Find everything you wanted?" he asked.

"And more."

"Ain't that always the way?" He looked past her.

Turning, she saw her friends approaching with their carts. Once their groceries were loaded with Hank's help, Sarah volunteered to return the carts to the store.

Miriam climbed in and sat on the rearmost seat. Leanna sat beside her, leaving the middle bench for her twin and Sarah.

After the van pulled out onto Main Street, they drove past several businesses, including a hardware store separated from the building next door by a narrow alley, a drugstore and several beauty salons and barbershops. Two diners faced off from opposite sides of the wide street. An empty area where a building had burned down five decades before was where a farmers and crafters market was held every Saturday. Miriam looked forward to being able to bring fresh vegetables to sell later in the summer.

They waited for the village's sole red light to change before turning left along East Broadway. Ahead of them was the old county courthouse, and the redbrick central school sat kitty-corner from it.

"*Danki* for asking me today," Miriam said with a smile. "I had a *wunderbaar* time and got some errands done, as well."

"We watched you having a *gut* time." Annie grinned. "Eli Troyer was intrigued with you."

"Don't be silly."

"Am I being silly?"

The other women shook their heads and laughed.

Deciding not to get caught in a game of matchmaking when she had no intention of making the mistake again of believing a man loved her enough to accept everything about her, Miriam said, "We should do things together more often."

"I agree." Leanna sighed. "I miss the youth group we belonged to several years ago at home."

"Here is our home now," Sarah said in her prim tone. "We've got to remember that."

Miriam wished Sarah would stop acting as if the twins were *kinder*. Maybe being around kids all the time, as Sarah was in her job as a nanny, made her speak so. Sarah needed to lighten up. Just as, Miriam reminded herself, she needed to.

"What shall we do for our next outing?" Annie's eyes twinkled. "We can be an older girls' club and have fun as the youth groups do."

Sarah nodded. "*Ja*, but I don't like calling ourselves 'the older girls' club.'"

"How about if we become a 'women's club'?" Leanna asked.

Annie shook her head. "Those are for married women. We aren't married. We're... What's the term? Not old maid. No. There's another one."

"Spinster." Miriam smiled. "Why don't we call ourselves the Harmony Creek Spinsters' Club? After all, a spinster is someone who helps take care of a home for her siblings and parents, which is what we do."

"I like it," Sarah said.

Leanna grinned as Annie jumped in with, "I like it, too. We'll be the Harmony Creek Spinsters' Club, and we can take turns choosing fun things to do together."

"Until we get married." Leanna wore a dreamy look. She was a romantic and devoured romance novel after romance novel.

Miriam wanted to warn her not to be so eager to make a match, but how could she when she'd been glancing out the window every few seconds, looking for a glimpse of the Troyer buggy? *I'm concerned if the little boy is all right.*

She chided herself for telling herself lies. She needed to listen to the advice she would have liked to offer Leanna. A desperation to get married could lead to dreadful mistakes. It was better to trust God's timing. Maybe if she'd done that, she wouldn't have jumped to accept the proposal of a man who'd seemed more interested, in retrospect, in having her raise his *kind* than anything else.

But no matter. She wasn't going to make such a mistake again.

Chapter Two

Kyle tugged on Eli's sleeve, trying to get his attention.

His nephew had been doing that for the past ten minutes while their buggy headed north along the main road that ran through the center of the village. They'd passed several fallow farms and newer houses on smaller lots.

Pulling his gaze from the road, he glanced at the little boy. Kyle swung his arm toward the horse, arching his brows.

Where are we going?

Eli sighed. He and the little boy, his only living relative, had developed their own sign language after the accident that killed his nephew's parents. Kyle had been a *boppli*, so for him, Eli's hearing loss was a normal part of his life. However, Eli doubted he'd get used to it himself. Hours of prayers, railing at God for the deaths of his brother and sister-in-law, had given him no insight into why the accident had to happen. Nor had pleading or bargaining. He didn't understand why the retaining wall his brother was building had collapsed.

What had Eli missed? He'd pointed out places where Milan needed to strengthen the wall, and his brother said he'd done as Eli suggested. Eli was a carpenter, unlike his brother, who'd seldom thought of anything other than his dairy herd.

Guilt rose within him like a river of fire. In retrospect, maybe he hadn't been as focused on the wall as he should have been. The day of the wall's tragic failure, too many of his thoughts had been about how he'd ask Betty Ann that evening to be his bride. He hadn't been sure she'd accept his proposal because he'd noticed her eyeing a couple of other guys, so nerves had plagued him. Distracted, he must have missed what brought the wall down on them.

When Kyle yanked on his sleeve, Eli wondered how long he'd been lost in thought.

"Let's go home," Eli said, checking the road before he made a U-turn.

The little boy frowned. Kyle probably thought his *onkel* had parted company with his mind.

And maybe Eli had because he'd driven out of his way to avoid having to see Miriam and her companions when their van zoomed past the buggy. It wasn't as if she'd strike up a conversation then. His efforts to avoid talking with his new neighbors had been successful so far, but church was the day after tomorrow. He couldn't avoid them there, though the *Leit* in Delaware had become accustomed to him and Kyle leaving right after the service and before the meal was served.

He wouldn't skip the gathering to worship together, but he dreaded seeing people bend toward each other to whisper as he passed. As if he were blind as well as almost deaf. More than once, he'd been tempted to shout that they could yell, and he wouldn't hear everything they were saying. He also hated the pitying looks aimed in his direction. Each one was a reminder of the expression Betty Ann had worn the first time she came to the hospital to see him after the accident. The first and only time she'd visited him there.

Would Miriam Hartz look at him the same way? The idea that such a lovely woman, who'd stepped in to defend a little boy she didn't know, would regard him as a victim of sorry circumstances twisted his stomach.

He was glad when Kyle demanded his attention again by pointing out sheep in a field they passed. He didn't want to think about seeing sympathy in Miriam's eyes.

God, give me strength.

He hoped this prayer would be answered before Sunday.

"Got a minute?"

On Saturday afternoon, Miriam looked up from her sewing machine.

Her brother walked into the barn that served as their home while he worked to make the farmhouse livable. The pipes in the house had frozen, and water spread through it, ruining floors and walls.

The barn was a single open space. Upon their arrival, she and Caleb had strung a web of ropes halfway to the rafters. Hanging quilts on the ropes had created rooms, including the private spaces where they slept. She'd placed rag rugs on the uneven floorboards to protect their feet from splinters. A propane camp stove allowed her to cook, and a soapstone trough became their kitchen sink. She and Caleb missed cakes, bread, cookies and everything else prepared in an oven. He'd picked out the double ovens he intended to put in the house. Until then, it was rough living, but with the doors and windows open, including the ones at either end of the loft, the space was comfortable at last. She'd thought they might become human icicles during the coldest days of the winter.

Turning off the sewing machine that got its power from a car battery, she made sure the half-finished purple dress was folded before she stood.

"What do you need, Caleb?" she asked.

"A favor." He sat at the table in the center of the open area. "Please hear me out before you give me an answer."

"Of course." She slid onto the bench facing him.

"I received a letter yesterday from the local school district. They'd written it at the request of the state education department."

She clasped her fingers together on the table. "Why?"

"They're concerned our *kinder* haven't attended school the minimum days for the school year."

"Mercy Bamberger has been homeschooling her two, and Nina Zook taught her four *kinder*."

"But there are four other families with *kinder* in our settlement. The state insists they attend the minimum number of school days."

"Do they have a suggestion of how we should do that?" Her brows lowered as she said, "If we'd had a school here, by now our scholars would be done so they can work on their families' farms."

"They suggested—and the local school superintendent, Mr. Steele, agreed—we hold school here for the next four weeks. That would take us to the middle of July, so the older scholars would be available to help with the harvest. At the end of the term, the *kinder* would be tested to make sure they'd learned what's mandatory for their ages."

She leaned toward him. "I thought our schools were independent of interference from *Englischers*."

"They are, but as you know, the *kinder* need to attend for a minimum number of days." He gave her a small smile. "I'm sure I can talk Mr. Steele into not having the testing, as long as I assure him the scholars will be in school for four weeks."

"That sounds like a *gut* idea. We've got about ten *kinder* of school age, I'd guess."

"Nothing you can't handle."

"Me?" she managed to choke out past her shock.

He didn't look at her as he said, "I sort of volunteered you because nobody else in the settlement has been a teacher."

"What about Mercy or Nina?"

"Mercy has her hands full with her foster son, and Nina is going to have her new *boppli* any day. You're our best choice to oversee the school."

Like everything else her brother did or said, it made complete sense.

But teaching? *Kinder* who'd be put into her care for six hours each day? She stared at him. How could Caleb ask such a thing of her? She'd come to Harmony Creek to escape the murmured accusations she couldn't be trusted with *kinder*.

"It's for only four weeks, Miriam," he said. "By the time school starts in the fall, Nina has said she'll take over until we can find a teen girl to teach. Just four weeks."

"All right, I'll do it." What else could she say? She

had to help keep the new settlement from getting off on the wrong foot with their *Englisch* neighbors.

"And I need you to do one other thing for me."

"I thought you said *one* favor."

"I guess I should have said one at a time."

She laughed with him. As hard as Caleb was working to make the settlement a success, he must be learning, at last, that he couldn't do it all himself. Though he continued to try.

"We're having a school built, so we'll be ready to go in the fall," he said. "It'll be between our farm and Jeremiah Stoltzfus's. There's a level piece of ground with not too many trees that will be perfect. We've hired a carpenter."

"What do you need me to do?"

"He's never built a school before, and you know what's needed."

"Our schools are pretty much the same."

"*Ja*, the ones in Lancaster County are. But schools in Indiana sometimes have two rooms and two teachers."

"Is that what you're planning on here?"

He shook his head. "The majority of our families are from Pennsylvania, so we're building what we're used to." His cheeky grin returned. "And one room is cheaper than two."

"True." She couldn't believe she'd agreed to be responsible for almost a dozen *kinder*.

"Will you work with him on the project?"

"Of course."

"*Gut.*" He pushed himself to his feet, came around the table and gave her a quick hug.

"Who's going to build the school?"

"Eli Troyer." Her face must have betrayed her shock,

because Caleb added, "I know it'll be a challenge to work with him."

She hadn't mentioned yesterday's incident at the grocery store to Caleb, because she'd been so busy she'd forgotten until after her bedtime prayers. "His nephew—"

"Shouldn't be around more than any other kid."

Hating the sympathy in her brother's voice, Miriam loved him at the same time for worrying about her. He did understand. She'd wondered whether Caleb would have invited her to join him in northern New York if circumstances in Pennsylvania had been different.

"Having kids around seems to be a given." She was shocked at the bitterness in her voice. She wasn't angry with her brother, but she was dubious of being in charge of the scholars. What if one of them got hurt?

Caleb's face lengthened with dismay. "If you don't want to—"

"I said I would, and I will."

"*Danki.* We should have the school done before the month is over. This weekend we're going to get the walls up and the roof on. Eli will cut in the windows and doors and finish the interior." This time her brother misjudged her hesitation because he went on, "I realize Eli has trouble hearing. I speak slowly, and he gets most of what I'm saying."

She thought of how his nephew seemed to be helping him comprehend what was being said. "How bad is his hearing? Really?"

Caleb shrugged. "Enough to be frustrating to him, I'd guess."

With a wave, her brother left.

She stared after him. If he'd told her first that she'd

be working with a man who had a *kind* the same age as Ralph Fisher, would she have agreed to assist with the school? She wasn't sure.

Eli was paying more attention to Miriam than he was to their temporary bishop Wayne Flaud, who'd come to oversee the service at the farm owned by the Kuhns brothers. How had Miriam reacted when Caleb told her that she'd be working with him? Had she been as astonished as he'd been?

Those were questions he couldn't get answered unless he asked her. He wouldn't put her in an embarrassing situation.

She was as lovely as he'd recalled over and over during the past two days. Her eyes weren't sparking as they had when she'd defended his nephew. Seated with the other young women who'd been at the grocery store, she looked at her clasped hands or the bishop who spoke at one end of the benches that faced each other. He could re-create her eyes' rich green shade. Even while sitting, she towered over the women around her. He was amazed such a tall woman could be so graceful in every motion.

And, when he'd thought nobody would notice, he'd been watching her every motion since she'd stepped out of her brother's buggy.

The bishop's voice, raised as he asked everyone to pray, intruded into Eli's thoughts. As he moved to kneel, facing the bench where he'd been perched, his eyes cut to her again.

He got caught, because his gaze connected with hers. For a single heartbeat before she turned to kneel. It'd been enough for him to confirm she'd been surprised by her brother's suggestion they work together. He didn't see dismay, though.

Lord, please make this collaboration a gut *one so the work we do together is a reflection of the hopes of this settlement.*

Keeping his prayers focused on the future was the best way to avoid thinking about the past and another pretty woman who'd dumped him like yesterday's trash. He glanced at his nephew beside him. He owed his brother and sister-in-law a huge debt for failing to protect them, and he intended to repay it, in part, by raising their son as they would have wanted.

Eli kept reminding himself of that obligation as the service came to an end. He needed to make a comfortable home for the little boy and earn a living to put food on their table. Once he finished, he'd look for more work.

As he'd done in Delaware, he made an excuse to avoid staying for the meal. If he met his neighbors one by one, he'd be able to get to know them well enough to guess what they were saying. In a crowd of almost thirty people, picking out individual voices and words was impossible.

Kyle looked disappointed as he glanced at the other *kinder*, but he didn't protest.

Eli draped an arm over his nephew's shoulders, surprised again at how much the little boy had grown in the past year. He'd inherited the Troyer height, and if he kept shooting up as he was, he'd be taller than Eli by the time he was a teenager. When they reached their buggy and Kyle climbed in, the little boy leaned forward and grabbed onto the sleeve of Eli's black *mutze* coat.

Astonished, Eli asked, "What is it?"

Someone talk to you.

"Who?"

The little boy pointed in the direction they'd come.

Eli's next question went unasked when he saw Miriam standing behind him, about ten feet away. By herself. Her friends were putting food on the tables set in the grass. Knowing he shouldn't be paying attention to such details, he couldn't help noticing how Miriam's dress was the exact green of her eyes. Her white *kapp* glistened as light sifted through the heart-shaped top, and her apron of the same shade seemed to glow in the sunshine.

She said something as she walked toward the buggy.

He assumed it was a greeting because she gave him a polite smile.

"I know Caleb wants us to work together," he said.

She blinked, and he guessed she'd expected him to chat about the weather or the church service before getting to the subject of the school. She couldn't know how difficult it was for him to make small talk.

"Ja," she said.

So far, so good.

"Miriam, I want to say *danki* for what you did at the store."

"You already..."

He hoped she'd said something about him previously thanking her for helping Kyle.

"It means a lot to me for someone to come to my nephew's defense as you did."

"...little boy, and he...nothing wrong." He was surprised when Miriam peered past him and into the buggy.

"Looking for something?" he asked. Too loudly, he realized when she winced.

After four years he should be used to that reaction from people when his voice rose with the strength of his emotions. He wasn't.

"I was...no matter."

Or at least that was what he thought she said as she stepped aside as Kyle jumped out of the buggy and gave her a big grin. Her expression grew uncertain and wary.

Of his nephew? Why?

Unsure how to ask that, he said, "I don't know if Caleb told you my nephew is living with me. His name is Kyle. He'll be one of your scholars. School starts next week, ain't so?"

When she forced a smile, it looked as if her brittle expression could shatter. She seemed to shrink into herself, acting as if she were allergic to Kyle and him.

He thought again about how she'd jumped to his nephew's defense at the grocery store. Why had she changed from that assertive woman—too assertive, many would say, for a plain woman—to a meek kitten who acted afraid of her own shadow?

"If you want to play ball with the *kinder* for a few minutes, Kyle," he said, "go ahead. Just come when I call you."

Kyle punched the air and ran off to join a trio of other boys and two girls near his age.

Knowing he should keep an eye on his nephew, though there were plenty of adults around, Eli couldn't stop his gaze from shifting toward Miriam again and again. She stared at Kyle and the other *kinder* as if they were a nest of mice about to invade her home.

Shock rushed through him. Why would Miriam Hartz agree to teach the settlement's *kinder* if she didn't like kids? Hadn't Caleb told him that she'd been a teacher in Pennsylvania? He had missed something, something her brother said or she did. No Amish woman who stood up for a little boy as she had displayed such an undeniable distaste for *kinder*. Why had she cringed away from Kyle?

As she noticed him appraising her, she said something he didn't hear and hurried toward the house and her friends. He'd better figure out her odd actions if there was any chance of Miriam and him working together successfully. He wished he knew where to begin looking for an explanation for her peculiar behavior.

Chapter Three

Miriam stood by the window offering the best view of
the rolling foothills of the Green Mountains at the horizon. When she'd first arrived at the Harmony Creek
farm, the hills had been a sad gray brown. The bare
trees had grown thick with leaves and bushes until the
hills looked as if they were covered with tight green
wool.

Closer were the neat rows of her gardens. Caleb
had rototilled two beds for her as soon as frost left
the ground. She put in seeds and the immature plants
she'd started in the cold frame. The simple wooden box
topped by glass acted as a miniature greenhouse. Using
it added to the time the plants could grow, which was
important when the growing season in northern New
York was short. Now in June, the plants were thriving
in the earth.

With a chuckle, Miriam tossed her dust rag on the
table and checked that her simple blue kerchief was
in place over her hair. Why was she inside on such a
beautiful day? School was starting at the beginning of
the week—the reason why she'd been trying to get her

weekly chores done today—so she wouldn't have as much time to enjoy her garden.

She glanced around the large space with its quilt walls. The ones hanging as "bedroom doors" had been pulled aside to let air circulate. It was strange to live in a place like this one, but it was beginning to feel like home.

As she walked outside, she thought of how truly blessed she was. She had *gut* friends, including those in the Spinsters' Club. She laughed. So far she hadn't shared the name and their plans to enjoy outings together with anyone else. She wondered what the reaction would be. Though she'd considered mentioning it to Caleb, she hadn't. He was so solicitous of her, and she wondered if he would think she'd lost her mind amidst her desolation about the canceled wedding.

The grass beneath her bare feet was as soft as the breeze making loose strands dance around her face. She curled her toes into the grass and drew in a deep breath as she watched Comet, their dappled-gray buggy horse, rolling like a young colt in the pasture. He was taking advantage of the day as she was.

Pausing to pluck a couple of weeds out of the flower bed to the right of the barn door, she glanced at the battered farmhouse. It was two stories high, but the roof dropped low over eyebrow windows. Caleb had replaced missing slats on the roof and installed drywall inside the house. Because he'd had to remove everything to the studs, he'd asked her to redesign the first floor. She'd made the kitchen bigger and added a mudroom and laundry room with a door to the yard, so it'd be easier to take laundry out to the line that ran from the house to the biggest barn. He'd put a movable wall between the two front rooms. That way, when it was their turn to host church, the wall could be shoved against the kitchen wall, making enough room for the *Leit*.

The outer walls would be painted white, and he'd agreed the shutters should be the same dark green as the shadows beneath the pine trees. The barns were a worn red, and he'd have to repaint them, too, but for now he was concentrating his scarce free time on the house.

Miriam admired the buds on the daylilies. They soon would be blooming. She planned to transplant her perennials along the front porch, and the best time for moving daylilies was August. She could wait longer to shift the daffodils she'd found in the woods. For the first two days after she brought the bulbs closer to the house, a groundhog had dug them up. She'd convinced the irritating burrower to leave them alone by dousing the flowers with a liberal amount of chili powder mixed with water. The strong scent had kept the animal away…at least so far.

She squatted by the flower bed and went to work. Less than five minutes later, she heard buggy wheels rattling toward the barn. Wondering who was coming, she gathered the weeds she'd pulled. She tossed them onto the compost pile before she walked around the barn's corner. If someone was looking for Caleb, she'd have to admit she wasn't quite sure where he was. He'd had a long list of errands to do in Salem and in Cambridge, about ten miles to the south.

She stopped in midstep, surprised when Eli climbed out of the family buggy. Why hadn't he said anything yesterday about plans to stop by?

Her breath caught when his nephew hopped out behind him. The little boy looked around with the candid curiosity of a six-year-old, and he pointed to Comet. The horse wasn't a common color for buggy horses. If the little boy went into the pasture and frightened him, it could be—

Stop it!

She scolded herself for looking for trouble where there might not be any. She wanted to stop reacting to the sight of a young *kind*, thinking of things that could go wrong, but she couldn't. Kyle reminded her of Ralph Fisher. Both were spindly and all joints as their elbows and knees stuck out from their thin limbs while they grew like cornstalks.

Eli had noticed her dismay yesterday after the church service. Nobody else had, not even her friends in the Spinsters' Club. She needed to keep her feelings to herself to halt the questions from beginning again—such as why a teacher hated kids. She didn't hate them; she loved them. Because she loved them, she didn't want to be the one to put any in danger.

"Gut mariye," Eli called.

She waved to him and his nephew and waited for them to cross the yard to where she stood. A siren sounded from the main road, and she flinched.

Kyle did, too, and scanned in every direction to see what sort of emergency vehicle it was.

Eli kept walking as if nothing had happened.

How bad was his hearing?

It wasn't her business. However, the teacher in her was curious how he'd managed to get by with only his young nephew to clue him in. A few quick tests he wouldn't know were going on would tell her the extent of his hearing loss.

"I brought plans for the school," he said when he reached her. "Do you want to see them?"

"Ja." She didn't nod to confirm what she'd said. "Seeing them is a *gut* idea because you want my help, ain't so?"

His dark brows dropped in concentration. He must have heard some of what she'd said and was trying to piece it together. Wondering why he didn't ask her to repeat what she'd said more slowly, she sighed. Even her *grossmammi* had resisted help for years because of *hochmut*, but pride did nothing to help her escape the ever-narrowing walls of her world as her hearing continued to fail. Nor would it help Eli.

She spoke to Kyle. "There's chocolate pudding in the fridge. Go ahead and help yourself to some. Have some with a glass of milk, too, if you want."

"Can I, *Onkel* Eli?" he asked.

More confusion fled through Eli's eyes, but he nodded when the little boy made motions that must have conveyed the question without words.

Miriam bit her lip to keep from saying sign language had limits because it could be understood by a limited number of people.

When the little boy skipped to the door and disappeared inside, she saw Eli's distress before he could mask it. Didn't he realize that, with Kyle beginning school, he needed to learn a different way to communicate? He wouldn't be able to depend so much on the little boy.

"Let me show you the plan I sketched for the school," Eli said, motioning toward the barn.

Was he hoping to head inside where his nephew could give him hints about what was being said?

"It's such a nice day, ain't so?" She sat on the cement ramp's edge. It would be used to bring equipment into the barn, once it was no longer their home. "Let's go over what you've got out here."

She thought he'd object, but he opened a large sheet of paper and spread it across the ramp beside her. He stood so close, each breath she took was flavored with the scents of his laundry soap and bleach. Unlike her brother's, his white shirt pulled over his head and had a stand-up collar. The tab front closed with four small buttons. Beneath the cotton, the shadows of the muscles along his brawny arms drew her eyes.

She looked away. Eli Troyer was too handsome for her own *gut*. She wasn't Leanna Wagler, believing in the possibility of a storybook hero coming to sweep her off her feet and carry her off to a *wunderbaar* life.

"What do you think?" he prompted, looking at his drawing. "It's a rough sketch, but it should show you what I'm planning. Feel free to tell me changes you think will make the school better."

She looked at the page. It was far more than a rough sketch, she realized. He'd marked out on the floor plan how the desks for the scholars and another larger one for the teacher would be set. He'd drawn the interior walls as if she stood in the room and looked at each one. It allowed her to see where he intended to place the blackboard and the bulletin boards. A generously sized storage closet was in a back corner.

He pointed to the narrow rectangles in the walls. "Those are windows. The bigger ones with the dotted lines showing the space for each to swing open and closed are the doors. What do you think?" He tilted his head toward her.

All air vanished as she found her nose so close to his that the piece of paper would have barely fit between them. She couldn't move or blink when she raised her gaze to meet the blue-hot heat in the center of his eyes. Every emotion within him was powerful and uncompromising.

Somehow she gathered enough air to ask, "Do you have a pencil I can use? I want to make a small change."

"Ja." He groped in his pocket and pulled out a short ruler.

"Pencil," she repeated as she pantomimed writing. Once he'd looked away, she drew in a deep breath.

What was wrong with her? She couldn't remember feeling like that when she was with Yost, and she'd been in love with him.

When a pencil was placed in her hand, she realized she'd drifted away on her thoughts. She kept her eyes lowered and squared her shoulders before bending over the page. The sooner she was done with reviewing the plans, the sooner she could put space between her and Eli.

"I think there needs to be another window on either side of the door." She drew what she wanted on the drawing.

"What are those?"

"Windows." She gestured toward the barn. "Windows."

"I know what you meant." He shook his head. "Windows suck heat out of a building. If there are more windows in the school, you'll be using a lot more propane to keep the building warm."

"Two small windows won't make much difference."

"I've been a carpenter since I was fourteen, and

I've learned a lot in those seventeen years. One thing I learned is that extra windows means needing more fuel to keep the space warm. No more windows."

"But—"

"You can't change facts, Miriam, no matter how much you want to."

"The fact I know is *kinder* work better in a sunny place than one filled with shadows." She folded her arms in front of her. "My brother trusts me to know what to do. That's why he's having me work with you to design the school."

He frowned, and she wondered if he'd understood what she said. She realized he'd gotten a bit of it when he said, "*Ja*, sunshine and shadows. Like in a quilt."

"I'm going to talk to Caleb about this," she said.

At her brother's name, comprehension dawned in his eyes. "Discuss it with him if you want." He shrugged. "He'll tell you the same thing I have."

She looked away. "He'll agree with me." She added the silliest thing she could think of. "He does about blue flamingos."

When she got no reaction from Eli to her challenging words, she stood and walked behind him as if looking at the sketch from another angle.

"I will be celebrating when he agrees with me," she said.

Again no reaction.

She clapped her hands.

He glanced over his shoulder and frowned. "Why did you do that?"

His question proved he could hear sounds, which was more than her *grossmammi* had been able to in the three years before she died.

"I told you." She smiled.

Her expression unsettled him. His gaze turned inward, and she guessed he was trying to figure out what she might have said. The silence stretched between them, a sure sign he couldn't guess what she claimed she'd told him.

"Oh." He gathered himself and said with calm dignity, "If you've got no other comments about the school…"

As he bent to get the piece of paper, she cupped her hands to her mouth and called out, "I've got lots and lots of comments. I want to paint the floor yellow and the walls purple. I want—"

He spun and stared at her before she could lower her hands. Wide-eyed, he demanded, "What are you doing?"

She met his accusing stare. "Testing you."

"Pestering me? *Ja*, that's true."

"No!" She frowned at him. "Testing. With a *t*." She sketched the letter in the air between them.

"I'm not one of your scholars. You don't need to test me to find out what my reading ability is."

Folding her arms in front of her, she gave him a cool smile. "That's not what I was checking. If you want, I can teach you to read lips."

"What?"

She touched her lips and then raised and lowered her fingers against her thumb as if they were a duck's bill. "Talk. I can help you understand what people are saying by watching them talk."

When he realized what Miriam was doing, Eli was stunned. A nurse at the hospital where he'd woken after the wall's collapse had suggested that, once he was healed, he should learn to read lips. He'd pushed that advice aside, because he didn't have time with the obligations of his brother's farm and his brother's son. Kyle had been a distraught toddler, not understanding why his beloved parents had disappeared.

During the past four years he and his nephew had created a unique language together. Mostly Kyle had taught it to him, helping him decipher the meaning and context of the few words he could capture.

"How do you know about lipreading?" he asked.

"My *grossmammi*." She tapped one ear, then the other. "...hearing...as she grew older. We...together. We practiced together."

Kyle came outside and rushed to them when Miriam gestured. He wore a milk mustache, and chocolate pudding dotted his chin.

When she bent to speak to him, too low and too fast for Eli to hear, the little boy nodded and took the tissue she handed him. She motioned toward Eli as she straightened.

Wiping his mouth and chin, Kyle faced him. *Learn to read talking. What's that?* The puzzled boy looked from Miriam to him at the same time he made the rudimentary signs he used to help Eli understand others.

"I can help." She put her hands on Kyle's shoulders. "Kyle...grows up. Who will...you then?"

Who would help him when Kyle wasn't nearby? He was sure that was what she'd asked. It was a question he'd posed to himself. More and more often as Kyle reached the age to start attending school.

"How does it work?" he asked.

"You watch my lips. We start with simple words. It is how my *grossmammi*… I learned."

Watch her lips? Simple? He would gladly have spent days watching her lips. His gaze was drawn to those rose-colored curves too often. Now she was giving him the perfect excuse to stare at them…

He shook his head.

"You…no help?" she asked, and he realized she'd confused his refuting of his own thoughts as an answer to her kind offer.

Before he could answer, Kyle pulled on his sleeve and motioned, *Help you. Her help you.*

As his nephew pointed at Miriam and then at Eli, Kyle's signals couldn't have been clearer. Kyle wanted Eli to agree to the lessons.

Not for the first time, Eli thought about the burden he'd placed on Kyle. Though Eli was scrupulous in making time for Kyle to be a *kind*, sometimes, like when they went to a store, he found himself needing the little boy to confirm a total when he was checking out or to explain where to find something on the shelves. If he didn't agree to Miriam's help, he was condemning his nephew to a lifetime of having to help him.

That wouldn't have been what his brother would have wanted. Milan and his wife, Shirley, had expected their son to play with friends and go to school and learn to assume responsibility for the family's farm. The farm had been sold so he and Kyle could start over by Harmony Creek, but he could ensure his nephew had the chance to be a kid. Was Miriam the way God was answering his prayer for help? If so, he needed to agree.

"All right," he said. "You can try to teach me to read lips."

She gave him a nod and a gentle smile, not the superior one he'd worried she'd flash at him. "…next Monday. You and Kyle—" she pointed at his nephew and at him, matching Kyle's motions "—supper. After we eat…"

"All right."

"Tell me."

For a second he was baffled, and then he realized she wanted him to repeat what she'd said so she could be certain he'd grasped the meaning of her words. His confusion became surprise. Why hadn't he considered such repetition was an easy way to avoid mistakes?

"You invited Kyle and me to supper," he said. "After the meal, you'll start teaching me to read lips."

"Gut," she said as his nephew held his fingers in an okay sign. Satisfaction sparkled in her cat-green eyes as if she'd enjoyed a bowl of cream. "Be prepare…work."

He hoped he wasn't going to prove to be an utter failure as he'd been with helping his brother make sure the wall was safe. Miriam seemed so confident she could teach him. He didn't want to disappoint her when she was going out of her way to help him.

Kyle threw his arms around Miriam and gave her a big hug. He grinned, and Eli realized how eager the *kind* was to let someone else help Eli fill in the blanks.

"You'll have a *gut* time at school, ain't so, buddy?" Eli asked, trying to cover his trepidation at losing Kyle's help.

Kyle tensed. *No go. Go later.*

Eli knelt in front of his nephew. "You'll be fine. You're going to enjoy school."

When Miriam nodded and said something, Kyle looked dubious.

The little boy shook his head. *Stay together. Eli and Kyle. No go now.*

"You'll be fine," he repeated. "The day will go so quickly you won't realize it because you're having fun with learning and your new friends."

Kyle touched one ear, then the other.

It took every sinew of strength Eli had not to flinch. That was a signal he hadn't seen the little boy make often, but he knew what it meant. Kyle was scared something bad would happen, as it had to Eli and his parents.

"It'll be okay. Miriam will be watching over you so you don't have to worry about getting hurt, ain't so?"

He raised his eyes toward her, expecting her to confirm his words. Instead, Miriam eased out of the little boy's embrace, her smile gone. She said something, but Eli didn't get a single word. She rushed away, vanishing into the barn where she lived with her brother.

What had he said wrong? One minute she'd been working to convince Kyle that going to school was something he wanted to do. The next she was fleeing as if a rabid fox nipped at her heels. Was it the thought of being with the scholars? Again, Eli found himself wondering why anyone who was so uneasy around *kinder* was going to be the settlement's teacher.

He didn't have time to figure it out. He needed to calm his nephew. "Looks like we're both going to start school next week," Eli said, patting him on the back.

Kyle gave him a distracted nod and kept staring at the door Miriam had used. Why was he acting as oddly as she had?

Had what Miriam said upset the little boy?

"What did she say as she was leaving?" he asked

as he tucked the page with the school drawing into his pocket. "Did you hear what she said?"

He nodded.

"What was it?"

The little boy started to open his mouth, then clamped it closed. Shaking his head, he ran to the buggy and climbed in.

Eli sighed. Kyle had heard something he didn't want to repeat. It'd happened a few times before, and Eli had discovered how useless it was to badger the little boy again to help him understand. Kyle always found a way to avoid answering him.

But Eli now did have one answer. He wasn't going to come to regret his decision to let her teach him lip-reading.

He already did.

Chapter Four

Drying her hands, Miriam crossed the barn toward the open door at one end. The *beep-beep-beep* announced the delivery truck from the lumberyard backing toward where a dozen men and boys waited in eager anticipation. The school's concrete foundation had been poured and given time to cure. Now they would work together to build walls and rafters. Once they had the skeleton in place, Eli would install shingles, clapboard, windows and doors before he finished the interior.

Spending time with Eli while he finished the school wasn't going to be easy. Having his nephew hanging around was going to add to the stress, but she needed to get used to it because other *kinder* would be coming to the barn for school on Monday.

And, in the fall, though she wouldn't be the teacher, the *kinder* would arrive every day to the school right across the road from her house.

Her heart contracted with the pain that never went away. *Ach*, how she'd longed for the family she thought she and Yost and Ralph would be! Even if the Lord hadn't blessed her and Yost with more *bopplin*, they would have had the three of them.

Then it was all gone.

Tears welled into her eyes, but she dashed them away. Crying for what was impossible was absurd.

She'd been blessed when Caleb invited her to come with him to help build a new settlement. Their parents and four older siblings, who were well established in their lives, had remained behind in Lancaster County. God had brought her to this point. He must have a reason for it. She must have faith that someday she would understand, and she would be able to accept why her joy had been torn away.

"Gut mariye," called the irrepressible Annie as she peeked past the front door. "Anyone home?"

"Komm in!" Miriam was glad to push aside her uncomfortable thoughts.

Dwelling on the past was useless. Dreaming of the future was more fun, but just as useless. She needed to concentrate on the present where she'd found three *wunderbaar* friends.

It was time to put sorrow behind her. She had to believe God had something better for her, something she couldn't even imagine yet. Wasn't that what faith was all about? Believing God would get her through the rough times?

Annie bounced into the barn followed by her twin. "Are you ready for a Harmony Creek Spinsters' Club meeting?"

"I'm ready to enjoy a visit from you anytime. Are you here for a meeting?"

"Of course not." Leanna rolled her eyes as she untied her bonnet. "Sarah had to work today. But the men are

having a work frolic, so we decided we should, too."
She put a basket on the table. "It was Annie's idea."

"Why am I not surprised?"

"Because you know I have *gut* ideas?" Annie asked.

"No, *that* would be a surprise," her twin teased with
affection. Motioning after she set two more bags on the
table, she added, "*Komm* here, Miriam, and see what
we've been able to dig up."

Miriam wasn't surprised when the twins began to
unload schoolbooks and stack them on the table. Each
grade level was printed with a different color cover,
and she saw they had several for most grade levels. She
already had the teacher's editions. Caleb had packed
them, figuring someone would use them along Harmony Creek. She wondered if he'd assumed he could
persuade her to teach again…at least temporarily.

She tapped her cheek in thought. "We'll need work-
books. I wonder where we can order them."

"Is there a bookstore in the village?" Leanna asked.

"Not that I've seen, but Caleb may know where one
is."

"Or go to the library and order the books from a
computer there." Annie's eyes twinkled.

"I'm not sure the bishop would approve." Miriam
sat at the table and began to sort the books out by
grade. "Maybe Sarah could ask Mrs. Summerhays if
she knows where we can place an order without using
the internet."

Since her arrival from northern Indiana, Sarah had
been working as a nanny for the Summerhays family,
who lived almost two miles east along the road toward
Rupert, Vermont. There were four *kinder*, two preteens
and two much younger *kinder*. Sarah told them it was

what *Englischers* called a blended family. The parents had been married before. Miriam didn't know if death or divorce had led to the *daed* and *mamm* remarrying, and she didn't ask. She assumed Sarah knew, but her friend wouldn't carry tales about the family's private business.

Leanna opened a textbook and turned the pages. "Here's the address for the publisher. If Mrs. Summerhays doesn't have a suggestion, I can write to the publisher and ask how to order more books. In the meantime, the scholars may have to share."

"A *gut* lesson for them," Annie said. "And the lesson for us is that the men working on the schoolhouse are going to be grouchy if there isn't food waiting for them for dinner."

They laughed and got to work unpacking food from the baskets. Squeezing cold casseroles into the small refrigerator along with the dishes Miriam had prepared, they set the hot selections on the table atop towels so the wood wasn't scorched. More food would be arriving soon.

"Mercy promised to make nachos," Miriam said as she handed several more glasses to Annie.

"Your neighbor is Hispanic, ain't so?" Annie asked.

"*Ja*, but she told me she learned to make nachos from her adoptive *mamm*. Her adoptive *Mennonite mamm*."

That brought more laughter as they worked together.

"Before the others get here," Annie said, "we need to plan another event for the Harmony Creek Spinsters' Club." She giggled. "I love getting to spend time with you. What does your brother think of it, Miriam?"

"I haven't said anything to him about our club." Her

embarrassment faded when she saw the uneasy expressions on the twins' faces. "I guess you haven't, either."

"It sounds as if we're desperate to be married," Annie murmured.

"Or have given up." Leanna clasped her hands in front of her. "I believe there's a man out there who will fall in love with me."

"All you have to do is not be looking for him, ain't so?" teased her twin. "Isn't that what you say the heroines in your romance novels do?"

Color burnished Leanna's cheeks. "I know those are just stories, Annie. I like reading them."

"I do, too." Annie's face became almost the same shade as Leanna's. "But if the right man comes along…" She sighed. "I don't want to lose this friendship."

"Once a member of the Harmony Creek Spinsters' Club, always a member, ain't so?" Miriam laughed, so glad she could let her worries slide away at least for a short while. Between the *kinder* coming for lessons and having Eli across the road day after day, in addition to teaching him to read lips, *not* thinking about those hurdles was a blessing. "We could rename it—"

"No! Don't change its name." Annie leaned forward with clasped hands. "Please!"

"But if none of us has told anyone—"

"The next one we come up with could be worse." Annie shuddered.

Again, they shared a big chuckle.

"If you'd let me finish…" Miriam waited until they were listening again. "I suggest we rename our older girls' group the Harmony Creek Spinsters' and Newlyweds' Club."

Leanna brightened. "That's perfect."

"Do you have something to share, little sister?" asked Annie as she winked at Miriam. "Big plans for the fall?"

Taking pity on the younger woman, Miriam put her arm around Leanna's shoulder. "I thought brothers were awful about picking on their sisters, but I think Annie takes the cake."

"Did I hear someone say cake?" called a deep voice from the door.

Miriam started to turn to motion to her brother to come in, but her eyes were caught by how pale Leanna's face became.

The young woman clamped her lips closed, but her gaze followed every motion Caleb made as he sauntered into the room and greeted them. When he spoke to Leanna, color erupted anew into her cheeks.

Could Leanna have a crush on Caleb? And did he look and smile at Leanna a bit longer than he did Annie? Caleb had been gone in the evening a lot lately. Was he walking out with Leanna?

Coming to her feet, Miriam knew she shouldn't be speculating on such private matters. A couple who was seeing each other didn't make that fact public until their intentions to marry were published two weeks before their wedding.

"You don't have an oven here, do you?" asked Annie.

He shook his head. "And I miss baked goodies." He winked at Miriam.

Her brother didn't like anyone outside the family to know he was a far better baker than she was. She could make tasty food, but he managed to create treats that were delicious and spectacular-looking. She understood his reluctance to share his skills with others. Few plain men spent time in the kitchen unless necessary.

"I wanted to give you a head's up," Caleb continued as he snatched a cookie off the tray the twins had
brought. "We'll be ready for dinner in about a half hour.
Will that work for you?"

"Certainly." Miriam smiled. "Do you want to eat at
the school or here?"

"We're going to set planks on sawhorses out in the
yard. That way you can serve from here. Does that
work for you?"

"Perfectly."

The other women nodded.

As her brother hurried out to continue working, Miriam noticed Leanna wasn't the only one watching. Her
twin was, as well. Were they both interested in her *gut*-
looking brother, or was something else going on?

Miriam didn't have time to puzzle out an answer
as two more women came into the barn, carrying additional food for the midday meal. As they worked together to have the meal ready for the laborers across
the road, she didn't have a chance to think of much of
anything but the tasks at hand.

It was an excellent beginning.

Eli straddled the ridge board at the roof's peak as
if it were a horse. Looking at the level stretched out
before him, he smiled. The bubble in the center glass
of the lengthy tool was exactly in the middle. He held
his right thumb up. Those who'd been working on the
school cheered.

Handing the level to LaVon Schmelley, who'd moved
into the hollow from Pennsylvania a month or so before
Eli and his nephew arrived, Eli reached for his ham-

mer as he waited for the first sheet of plywood to be slid toward him.

LaVon squinted through his gold-rimmed glasses as he handed off the level to someone standing on the ground and guided the large sheet into place. Eli nailed the top into place with an air-powered nail gun. LaVon used a regular hammer on the bottom.

The other man grinned and said something Eli didn't catch; LaVon pointed to the ground. Eli looked down.

Caleb and Jeremiah Stoltzfus, whose farms shared a common border, motioned toward them. Eli couldn't guess what they were trying to communicate. When LaVon edged to the ladder while the other men put aside their tools and walked across the road, Eli guessed it was time to eat.

His stomach rumbled at the thought and tightened with anxiety. He hesitated while the men began lifting plywood on top of sawhorses. From where he sat, he could see Miriam working with a half dozen other women to arrange chairs around the makeshift tables.

He groaned, wishing he had some excuse not to join the communal meal. Unlike on church Sundays, he couldn't slip away. He was needed to oversee the afternoon's work. A quick glance at the ground warned he couldn't use needing to get more supplies as an excuse for why he couldn't sit with the rest of the workers while they ate.

Taking a deep breath, he climbed down. He took his time switching off the nail gun and the air compressor. Without its low rumble, he caught staccato hints of voices and laughter. No specific words, but he guessed the atmosphere was casual and cordial. He wished he could feel that way, too.

Pausing to wash his hands at the hand pump set between the barn and the dilapidated house, Eli walked to where a generous assortment of food was arranged on planks that would be used on the school's roof and walls. Drawing in a deep breath of the aromas, he helped himself to a variety of casseroles, a couple rolls and apple butter. Conversation buzzed like a swarm of maddened bees, and he picked out a few words. Enough to let him know most of the discussion was about the progress on the school.

He smiled. That he could talk about, though he wished Kyle was there. His nephew was *gut* about clueing him in to the specifics of anyone's comment.

Taking a seat at the end of one makeshift table, he said silent grace before digging into his food. It was as tasty as it smelled. He'd learned that bending over his plate and appearing completely focused on his meal kept others from trying to draw him into the conversation.

He couldn't keep himself from looking at where Miriam sat at a nearby "table." She was chatting with her friends, and they laughed with an ease that suggested they'd known each other their whole lives. He remembered when it'd been simple to be around people and enjoy their company, but that seemed as if it were part of someone else's life.

Suddenly, she looked in his direction.

And caught him watching her.

A piece of roll stuck in his throat, and he fought not to cough. It would draw everyone's attention.

Miriam will help you learn to understand others better.

He couldn't deny the truth, but spending time with her might only increase how often she invaded his thoughts. A bad idea. He couldn't see any outcome other than her dumping him as Betty Ann had or her trying to shower him with compassion. He didn't want either, especially the latter because he'd come to equate compassion with pity.

When Caleb called out what must have been a jesting comment because everyone laughed, Eli chuckled, too, though he had no idea what Caleb had said. He relaxed when he realized the topic was how he was looking to establish himself as a carpenter. Questions were fired at him, and he kept nodding, hoping he wasn't committing himself to something he didn't have the skills to do.

"...more pie?" asked Miriam as she held a plate out in front of him.

The aroma of baked apples flavored with cinnamon and nutmeg made his mouth water. He took the plate. *"Danki."*

"You...doing well."

"Ja, you'll be moving the scholars into the school before you end your summer term."

Her smile wavered as it did whenever he mentioned her teaching the *kinder.* Curiosity tugged at his tongue, urging him to ask the obvious questions.

He didn't.

If he started probing into why she acted as she did, she might do the same to him. He didn't want to talk about the tragedy...again and again as he'd had to in Delaware.

"You...rest doing a *gut* job," she said before she put another piece of pie in front of a man who'd been cutting two-by-fours.

In spite of himself, Eli's hand paused between the plate and his mouth while he watched the other men's gazes following Miriam. That wasn't any surprise, because she was lovely. What *was* a surprise was the swell of something distasteful when she wore a brilliant smile as she answered a man on the other side of the table.

Jealousy.

For the time she was spending with the others? Or for how easy it was for them to talk with her?

Or both?

Lord, help me focus on what's important for me and for Kyle.

It was a prayer he needed to keep in his heart every hour of every day.

Yet, it was impossible to look away when Miriam set a plate in front of LaVon, who was sitting across from him. She said something to the other man, but her gaze locked again with Eli's.

This time she didn't look away like a frightened rabbit. She met his eyes. The bits of voices he could discern faded as he became lost in the connection between them. Every instinct told him to tear his gaze away. He didn't.

Was it confusion he saw on her face? Was she as baffled and uncertain about this invisible bridge that spanned the distance between them?

Eli had no time to puzzle that out because she looked toward the other end of the tables. Just as everyone else did. Belatedly, he copied the others' motions.

Caleb had risen to his feet. He was smiling as he spoke, but Eli caught only two words.

"Fire department…"

He didn't know what else Caleb had said. Whatever it was must have been important because the other men were sitting back, considering Caleb's words. Eli waited for one or more of them to ask questions so he could discover why Caleb had mentioned a fire department.

"Volunteers…?" asked LaVon.

"Ja." Caleb smiled as he sat again and folded his arms on the table. When Eli strained, he picked out the words, "With more houses…Harmony Creek…more volunteers. We're here during the day. That…*gut* for the department."

Eli understood. Or hoped he did. The local fire department was looking for more volunteers, especially those who were at home during the day. From what he'd learned about Salem, most people worked in other towns, some driving more than thirty miles each way. A fire during the day would get out of control without enough volunteers to fight it. The arrival of the Amish who worked on their farms was the perfect solution to the quandary.

"Interested?" asked Caleb as he looked in Eli's direction.

"Ja. I volunteered in Delaware." He wished he hadn't jumped on the chance when he saw Miriam frown in his direction.

He understood what she didn't say. Kyle had told him about the sirens that had sped past on the main road, the ones Eli hadn't heard when he went to talk to Miriam about the schoolhouse plans. No wonder she looked puzzled that he was volunteering to be a firefighter.

As if she'd voiced her doubts, Caleb said, "We…pagers." He held up a small device before hooking it onto his belt. "They alert…and we go."

"Okay with Wayne?" asked Jeremiah.

"Ja," Caleb said.

Everyone began talking at the same time, and Eli

couldn't pick out more than an occasional word. Rising, he carried his plate to where a tub was filled with soapy water. He put it in and headed back to work.

He halted, almost rocking off his feet to keep from running into Miriam. She stared at him, silent.

"If you think," he said, deciding to speak plainly, "I can't be a firefighter because of my hearing loss, think again. Nobody can hear much of anything when a fire is roaring."

Her eyes narrowed. "But you need…hear if the fire… unexpected turn."

"If the fire goes in a different direction?" When she nodded, he added, "You sound as if you've had experience with a bad fire."

"How many of us haven't?" She glanced at the barn that was the Hartz family's home. "Lightning and barns…no mix."

"I don't know how bad lightning will be along our creek. I'd expect bolts would head straight for the water." His eyes swept the hills and mountains edging the horizon before focusing on her. "We're sited low compared to what's around us. That should keep us protected."

"Unless the storm is right over us."

He gave her a grim smile. "Looking for trouble means finding it. I'd rather have faith God will send the storms around us. It's not our place to tell Him what to do, ain't so?"

When he saw her flinch, he realized he was being too inflexible. She was concerned about his safety. He should appreciate that, and he did. But when she stood so close he had trouble thinking only about his nephew and their future.

"When…lessons…?"

She was asking about him learning to read lips. He wanted to tell her he'd changed his mind, that he was willing to go on as he had. He'd gotten by four years without the skill.

"Is Monday night still okay? *Komm* to supper," she said. "Lessons…after…" Not giving him a chance to answer, she walked away to help clear the table.

His gaze followed her until he realized others were watching him watch her. Turning on his heel, he strode toward the school's framework.

Miriam might be able to teach him to read lips, but he'd learned a tough lesson from his ex about trusting women. It was one he'd be a *dummkopf* to forget.

Chapter Five

Miriam stood in the barn door as she had in the Lancaster County schoolhouse door when she'd been the district's teacher. She didn't have a bell to ring, but the moment she'd opened the door, the boys and girls began running across the yard toward her. She hadn't guessed they'd be eager to spend summer mornings doing schoolwork.

The day was humid, so maybe they preferred sitting inside to working in the fields or weeding in the garden. The big barn, which had been so cold during the winter, seemed resistant to letting heat in. For that, she was grateful.

She silently counted as she greeted each *kind* coming through the door. Ten students. Half the number she'd had in Lancaster County, and most of the scholars were between the ages of six and nine. That would give her more time with each group while they concentrated on doing the work the state education department deemed necessary.

Caleb was discussing the need for end of term testing with the local school superintendent. Miriam hoped her suggestion that each scholar do a special project would be acceptable rather than requiring the *kinder* to take day-long tests in the middle of July's heat. Her brother intended to share that plan with Mr. Steele at their meeting next week.

"Find a seat at the table," Miriam said with the best enthusiasm she could gather.

Her hands shook as she walked to one end of the table where she'd set a whiteboard Caleb had found for their impromptu classroom. She hoped the *kinder* wouldn't notice her trembling fingers, and, if they did, they'd think she was nervous about teaching.

Ten young faces looked in her direction. Her heart swelled with affection for the little ones who were the future of their new settlement.

She could do this. She could keep them safe for six hours each day. Each *kind* was being picked up that afternoon. Their parents had agreed to come to collect them, so she'd confirm which routes the *kinder* would take to and from the school. That way she could keep an eye out for them in the morning and make sure they left in the proper directions in the afternoon. Knowing she was watching might keep a few of them from getting into trouble as Ralph and his friends had.

"Shall we start our morning with a song and a prayer?" she asked.

As the scholars replied with enthusiasm, she thanked God for the routine that had served her well in the past. She sang with the *kinder*, loving the sound of their treble voices brightened by their smiles. In spite of everything, she was grateful for a chance to spend time with them. She was sure, with His help, she could get through the next four weeks. Then she'd hand the teaching job over to Nina and find a way to be busy every morning and afternoon in a part of the house that didn't have a view of the school or the *kinder*.

Cutting herself off from the scholars would break her heart. But if Yost had been right and she couldn't be trusted with kids, it was for the best.

The next evening Miriam took the warm strawberry pie Mercy Bamberger held out to her and thanked her in *Englisch* and *Deitsch*. Mercy, who lived on the farm next door, gave her a grateful smile. Her neighbor was struggling to learn the language so she could become a full member of the community when she was baptized in the fall. In addition, the woman, who'd been raised as a Mennonite, worked to understand the High German used at the Sunday services. She was making *gut* progress, and her *kinder* were speaking *Deitsch* as if they'd used it their whole lives.

"Are we the last ones to get here?" Mercy asked as her daughter and son went to join the other *kinder* who were kicking a ball around the far end of the barn.

Once the discussion on their new *Ordnung* began, the youngsters would take their game outside between the barn and the house, out of the way of buggies driving into the farm. Caleb had looked at Miriam with sympathy when she made that suggestion. Though her brother was well aware of everything that had been said in Lancaster County, he'd never questioned her assertion that she hadn't realized she was supposed to watch Ralph before he arrived.

He'd been the only one.

Shaking those thoughts from her head, Miriam said, "No, you're not the last. Eli and Kyle haven't arrived yet."

Why, when he'd been understanding about the near-tragedy in Pennsylvania, had Caleb been oblivious to her frustration when he'd shifted the settlement's weekly Tuesday meeting to tonight? She was supposed to start teaching Eli to read lips tonight, but he wouldn't want to begin the lessons when so many others were gathered in the barn.

Nor did she want to teach him while they had an audience. Her *grossmammi* wouldn't have cared who was there. She'd been so eager to learn. Eli was suspicious of the whole process and didn't think it would help him much. She wasn't sure why he was reluctant. If their situations had been reversed, she was certain she'd want to try anything and everything that might help her "hear" again.

"Paul will be disappointed to hear that," Mercy said, drawing Miriam out of her thoughts. "He was looking forward to seeing Kyle."

Miriam nodded. The two boys spent every possible minute together at school. "It's too bad they live at opposite ends of the hollow."

"They'll be able to get together when they're older and know to watch out for cars along the road."

As if to emphasize Mercy's words, wheels squealed around a turn in the road outside the barn. Everyone stopped talking and exchanged uneasy glances.

"Maybe we should talk to the sheriff sooner rather than later about how fast cars go along this road," Sarah's brother Menno said with a scowl. "I know you want to wait until you've had a chance to discuss this with Wayne, Caleb, but someone's going to get hurt or killed."

As she set the pie on the table with the other food

brought by the members of the settlement, Miriam watched her brother debate with himself. He was distressed when *Englisch* teens drag-raced and when their parents drove too fast. The road with its curves and hills and dips made it impossible to see far ahead. But he was bothered more by everyone looking to him as if he was the bishop. The settlement needed to ordain two of the married men to become their first minister and deacon. Those men would then oversee the *Leit*, but that wouldn't happen until the communion service in the fall.

When Eli and Kyle walked in, Caleb looked relieved that he didn't have to answer right away.

The boy grinned and waved in Paul's direction. Miriam wondered if anyone else noticed the odd motions the boy made to his *onkel* before Eli nodded, and Kyle skipped across the barn to join the other *kinder*.

Menno called, "Eli, did you see the speeding car?"

She held her breath, eager to discover how much he'd understood. When he took his time to reply, no one else seemed to think it was unusual. Many plain people had developed the habit of answering every question after what *Englischers* in Lancaster County called "an Amish pause." Perhaps it was another reason Eli had been able to function with his severe hearing loss for so long.

"Cars," Eli responded. "Two of them. They were racing. Praise the *gut* Lord we'd already turned onto your lane, Caleb, when the cars came around the corner. If we'd been on the road…" He didn't finish.

He didn't have to. Every plain person understood the peril of a collision between a car and a buggy. The results were almost always the same. There would be damage to both vehicles, but the passengers in the buggy had only a thin layer of fiberglass and wood between them and a steel-reinforced car. The *Englischers* might be injured if they hit the horse, but the plain people were often killed.

Jeremiah sighed. "Menno, I think your suggestion about contacting the authorities right away has a lot of merit."

Miriam watched everyone turn to Caleb. She admired how he'd shouldered the burden without complaint, but he seemed more weighed down every day. She wished there was something she could do to help him. Maybe—and she looked to where Eli had found a seat among the other men—teaching Eli to read lips would help. Eli was a man who considered his thoughts before he spoke. Such a man would be able to ease Caleb's load.

There was a single empty chair among the women who'd brought their mending and other sewing to do while the men debated. As soon as she sat, she realized Eli was in her line of sight. She couldn't move as her friends exchanged mirthful glances. Later she'd explain to them—again!—that she wasn't interested in Eli, other than as her student.

Don't be false with yourself, cautioned her conscience.

She realized she'd flinched in response to that thought when Annie leaned over and whispered, "Are you okay?"

"Ja." Miriam offered her friend a smile.

It must have been believable because Annie nodded and grew quiet as the *kinder* hurried outdoors and the men began their meeting.

The topic was buggies. Or it was supposed to be,

which was why Miriam was surprised to hear Caleb say, "That's why my sister has been concerned about where the scholars travel to and from the school."

Had someone complained about her questions to the scholars' parents earlier? If so, why hadn't they spoken to her? She would have been happy to explain, though she wouldn't have shared why she was concerned.

Eli's gaze caught hers, erasing the distance between them. He shook his head.

What did he mean? It was odd to be trying to figure out what he was attempting to communicate rather than the other way around.

When he gave her a smile and a wink, she almost gasped. How could he be so bold when everyone was around them?

Then she realized nobody else had paid attention to her and Eli staring at each other…for how long?

Two youngsters ran into the barn, one holding out a bloody finger. She jumped to her feet and rushed to get her first-aid kit. In quick order she had the two boys, who were among the oldest in her makeshift school, seated while she tended to the finger as well as the other youngster's scraped knee. She stepped aside when their *mamms* came to comfort them.

And her eyes locked again with Eli's. Had he been watching her the whole time? A startling warmth swept over her. Not embarrassment, but something sweeter. Something she'd vowed not to feel again. She didn't want to be drawn to another man, especially one with a *kind*.

She looked away. She must not put herself into another situation where she would prove to be a disappointment to someone she cared about.

* * *

While Miriam returned to her chair among the other women, Eli turned to look at the gathered men. They'd drawn chairs closer for the discussion. He was relieved the women wouldn't join the conversation. Otherwise, he would have had to swivel to try to catch what they said. It was difficult enough to guess which man would speak next.

"Tonight's topic for our *Ordnung*," Caleb said, "is buggies. Color and style."

Eli wasn't surprised Caleb wanted to start with an item that was vital to the identity of the settlement. Because families had come from multiple districts and states, there were different types of buggies in use. Eli's from Delaware was black and squat. LaVon Schmelley drove one with the bright yellow top that was used in western Pennsylvania. Sarah's brothers had a black Indiana buggy. The rest of the ten families living in the new settlement drove the gray-topped buggies seen in Lancaster County.

Deciding on the new settlement's buggy style wasn't simple. Once a unanimous decision was made and the bishop concurred, the families driving nonconforming buggies would have to purchase new ones. Each could cost $5,000 or more.

Menno suggested that they continue to drive their current buggies until after the crops were harvested in the fall. Each farm could put a share of their crop profits into a central fund to purchase buggies for those families who would need new ones.

"Once we know how many we'll need to replace," Eli said, "we might be able to work a deal because we'll be ordering more than one. Selling the ones we don't need could help raise the funds, too."

"That's true." Caleb glanced around the circle before his gaze settled again on Eli. "...buggy maker?"

Why hadn't he kept his mouth closed? Now he was part of the conversation, and Caleb, being the fair man he was, intended to keep him included.

Before Eli could figure out what to say when he didn't understand the question, Menno asked, "Sarah, didn't you... Mr. Summerhays...connection to the horse racing in Saratoga?"

She nodded, looking up from the shirt she was mending.

Menno turned to the men again, making it easier for Eli to hear him. "Mr. Summerhays is the man my sister works... He and his business partners own...racing horses. The...harness track...small-wheeled vehicle...sulky. Someone builds...sulkies. Why couldn't... buggies?"

As the others continued to discuss the issue, Eli looked at where the *kinder* were again playing with a ball in a corner. They must have returned inside after the two were hurt. He was glad to see they were far enough away from the area Miriam and Caleb used for their home, so there wasn't any chance something would be broken.

Someone tapped on his arm, and Eli returned his attention to the conversation. What had he missed?

As if he'd asked that aloud, Caleb said, "Eli...your buggy."

Eli had no idea what Caleb wanted to know. Was he asking about Eli's buggy or had he been talking about something else altogether?

"A moment," he said as he waved toward his nephew. Trying to piece together what everyone was talking about was impossible without help.

Kyle handed another *kind* the ball he was holding and trotted toward Eli. When the boy exchanged a glance with Miriam, Eli didn't have to guess to know what they were thinking. Miriam's expression was sympathetic and Kyle's resigned.

Guilt surged through Eli as the boy stopped beside him. He was torn. He wanted his nephew to have a chance to play like the other kids, but without Kyle's help, he'd be lost. If he'd started lipreading lessons with Miriam by now... But he hadn't, and he needed the boy's help.

Eli was able to follow the conversation better with Kyle's assistance. No one asked why he'd brought his nephew into their circle. Several times he caught Kyle glancing wistfully toward the far corner. The guilt gnawing at Eli grew.

When a decision was reached on the color and style of the buggies to be part of their *Ordnung*, Eli wasn't surprised. Most of the families drove gray buggies, so it'd be easier for the community to help pay for replacement buggies for the few families who didn't. Eli surprised himself by entering the conversation again to say instead of selling the nonconforming buggies, they find someone to strip them and turn them into open buggies teenage boys drove during their *Rumspringa*.

When the meeting broke up after dessert and *kaffi*, Eli went to where Miriam was gathering paper plates and cups. The families were using disposable dishes until they could purchase enough china and flatware for the whole settlement on a church Sunday. His buggy might be reconfigured into a bench wagon to move the supplies from house to house every other week. Few changes would be necessary, because the axles were wide enough to support a vehicle that would hold plenty of benches and dishes.

"Is...wrong?" he heard Miriam ask.

He shook his head. "No. Why do you think there's something wrong?"

"You're frowning."

"Just thinking." He explained how his buggy could be put to use.

She gave him a faint smile. "Tell Caleb about... It... *gut* solution."

"Ja." Without a pause, he asked, "When can we begin lipreading lessons?" He couldn't forget the glance Miriam and Kyle had thought nobody else had noticed.

"It's late tonight."

"It is."

"Tomorrow...ain't so?"

Praying he'd understood her, because it wasn't easy concentrating on listening to her when he couldn't stop wondering if her skin was as smooth as it appeared, he replied, "Tomorrow is *gut.*"

Relief blossomed in her pretty eyes, and he was amazed. Why was she determined to help him? He was pretty much a stranger.

Then he saw her turn to smile at Kyle. A genuine smile, and Eli wondered if she'd offered to help him because of his nephew. And why that made him relieved and hurt at the same time.

Chapter Six

When he heard Eli and Kyle were coming to the barn the following evening, Caleb had told Miriam he'd be willing to stay instead of painting the kitchen in the house. He was eager to get to work, because he wanted the house ready for them to move into as soon as possible. Neither of them wanted to spend another winter in the drafty barn. Jeremiah had offered to help him tonight. The two men also, she suspected, would be talking about removing the fences along their shared property lines, so they could work the small fields more efficiently. The fewer times the teams had to turn at the end of each row, the more quickly the field could be plowed and harvested.

Miriam had urged her brother to work on the kitchen as he'd planned. She didn't need to be chaperoned. After all, the little boy was coming along with his *onkel*. She was glad because Kyle needed to learn, too, so he could help Eli practice.

She wasn't sure if Eli would be willing to have his lesson if Caleb was present. She'd seen his respect for her brother, and, though he had no reason to, Eli was disconcerted whenever he must admit his hearing loss was worse than others guessed.

That was what she kept telling herself as she waited for the Troyers to arrive. Yet, she couldn't ignore the truth. She was looking forward to spending time with Eli and having a chance to know him better.

He fascinated her. She sensed there were depths to the man he refused to allow anyone to see. Discovering what he hid could be foolish because she might, at the same time, reveal too much of what she wanted to put behind her. What would he think if he found out her betrothal had been broken after a *kind* had almost died because of her inattention?

Eli was so protective of his nephew, and, if he learned the truth about what had happened to Ralph, he might decide to pull Kyle out of school. That could create problems for Caleb with the *Englisch* school district. She must keep her past in the past so it wouldn't interfere with the future of the settlement…and her slow-growing friendship, if it could be called that, with Eli.

The aroma of fresh *kaffi* wafted through the barn as Miriam put chocolate chip and oatmeal-raisin cookies on a plate. She'd gone to the twins' house to make the cookies earlier. She'd set some aside for Caleb. Her brother missed having an oven as much as she did. Maybe more. Though he never spoke of it beyond their family, Caleb had been taught to bake by their *grossmammi*. As a boy, he'd hurried to finish his chores so he could assist *Grossmammi* Hartz in the kitchen.

Miriam smiled. The stove with double convection ovens had been delivered by a large truck earlier. Caleb had been as excited as the scholars at recess.

"Guten owed." Eli walked in, followed by his nephew.

Their expressions were wary as they took off their straw hats. She must make them feel comfortable straightaway, though she wondered why the boy was as leery of these lessons as his *onkel*.

"*Guten owed,*" she replied and motioned toward the table where the scholars sat during the school day. "You can put your hats on a chair. Caleb moved the pegs we have been using to the house. Help yourself to some cookies. *Kaffi*, Eli?"

She was no longer surprised he looked at his nephew before he answered. She'd seen he had a greater difficulty hearing women's voices than men's. She wasn't surprised because her *grossmammi*'s hearing loss had been much the same.

"*Ja,*" he said finally.

With a smile, she looked at the boy. "I've got lemonade, Kyle, but you probably don't want that with cookies. Milk?"

The boy nodded.

She went to get drinks for them and a glass of milk for herself while they sat beside each other at the table. With a smile, she set a cup in front of Eli and the milk by Kyle's clasped hands. She retrieved her own glass before sitting on the bench facing them.

"Shall we begin?" Miriam asked, knowing how Eli struggled, even with Kyle's help, to engage in small talk.

Both Troyers nodded as Kyle reached for a cookie.

Miriam took a deep breath. She recalled the simple techniques she'd learned at the beginning of her training with *Grossmammi* Hartz. She could still hear the first words spoken by the instructor, an *Englisch* woman who was almost as old as her *grossmammi*.

"You are learning to read lips," the instructor had

said. "It would be easier if the people around you learned, too. That is not going to happen. That is why you must find a way to function in any situation."

"How can I help my *grossmammi*?" Miriam had asked.

"Start by not using contractions or complex sentences. Follow the kiss rule by keeping it short and sweet." She'd smiled. "Kiss and lips go together."

Miriam remembered blushing, which brought laughter from the older women. But she hadn't forgotten.

She tapped her lips, drawing Eli's gaze toward them. "It is time to begin."

"Okay." His tone was dubious.

As if he was enthusiastic, she began to outline what she intended to teach him. She spoke slowly but not with exaggerated enunciation. Eli needed to learn to communicate with people who were talking normally. She would increase her speaking pace as his skills grew.

She began by pointing to common items and naming them. Eli and Kyle repeated them after her. She told Eli to look from her to Kyle as each of them took turns speaking. Following a conversation among multiple people was a tough skill to become proficient in, so she wanted him to practice right from the beginning.

Eli was more patient than she'd expected. That told her how desperate he was to be able to understand those around him. She hoped his resolve didn't falter as the lessons went on.

"Some words are confusing," Miriam said after refilling Eli's cup and Kyle's glass. "Like bat and pat." Making a pair of wings with her hands, she flapped them. "Bat." She tapped the table. "Pat. See? They look the same on the lips."

"Ja," Eli replied. "But if I can't understand such simple words, how can I learn the more difficult ones?"

She laughed. "The difficult ones are easier to understand because they are unique. See? No other word looks quite like *unique* when spoken." She repeated the word twice more.

"Unique is unique. Is that what you're saying?"

When she smiled, Kyle giggled and reached for another cookie.

"You must have a mirror in your house," Miriam said after taking a sip from her own glass.

Eli nodded. *"Ja,* I've got one for shaving."

She didn't look at the strong line of his jaw as she imagined him drawing a razor along it before he swept soap suds from his skin. Many times she'd seen her brother perform the daily task. Yet, the thought of Eli doing the same sent a warm shiver of something delightful through her.

Hoping he couldn't guess the course of her thoughts, she said as if she had nothing more on her mind than their lesson, "You should practice in front of the mirror."

"Practice what?"

"Reading lips."

"My own?"

"Ja. Put the mirror on the table while you and Kyle are eating. Prop it against something. Watch your lips move as you speak to him. *You* know what you are saying. Learn how your own words look. It will help you recognize the same words when others say them."

He didn't reply, and she could see he was trying to puzzle out what she'd said. She halted her immediate instinct to repeat herself. If she did without waiting for him to ask, she wouldn't be helping him.

"That makes sense," he said.

"But?"

"But what?"

"That is what I am asking you. You sound as if you are unhappy that I made a *gut* suggestion."

His eyes widened, and he shook his head. "I didn't mean that. My reaction didn't have anything to do with you. Just with me. I should have thought of doing these exercises myself."

"Why?"

Again, he looked at her, baffled. "I don't understand what you mean."

"I mean, why are you rebuking yourself for not figuring out what it took experts a long time to?"

"It's been four years since I could hear well." His mouth grew taut, and his eyes cut to the boy beside him before guilt washed over his face.

Instead of answering him, she smiled at his nephew. "Kyle, will you take these extra cookies to the house? Caleb and Jeremiah are there, and they would like a snack."

"Can I take some for me?" the boy asked.

"Two more."

He grinned, jumped from the bench and hurried out with the plate. She hoped the cookies would survive his eager lope across the yard.

Eli stood. "Where's he going?"

"To the house." She reached across the table and tapped a finger against his arm. When he focused on her, she repeated her answer before adding, "I sent him over there to Caleb and Jeremiah because I could tell you did not want to talk about when Kyle's parents died. Not while he was sitting right here."

"No, I didn't." He frowned. "How did you know?"

She motioned for him to sit again. When he had, she said, "It is another part of what you need to learn. You can get clues to what is being said by watching what people say with their motions and expressions."

"What?"

Realizing he hadn't caught enough of her words to comprehend what she was saying, she replied, "Body language. Do you know what that is?"

"*Ja*... No, not really. I've heard people mention it, but I don't know what they were talking about. Sorry."

"You do not need to apologize. I did not know what it was until I started helping my *grossmammi*." She smiled. "Not by name. I did not realize what I was sensing without realizing it." Getting up, she folded her arms and raised her chin. "Can you tell what I am feeling if I stand like this?"

"Proud?" he asked.

"Try again."

"Angry?"

"Closer." She gauged his expression and posture to make sure she didn't push him until frustration made him give up. After letting him guess two more times, she said, "I am defiant, an emotion you know well, because you refuse to accept your hearing loss."

He rubbed his chin between his finger and thumb as he considered her words. "And I look like that sometimes?"

"More often than you would guess. Crossed arms are a signal the person wants to keep you at bay. Rais-

ing your chin means you refuse to be moved by anyone else's words."

His eyes brightened, a sure sign he understood. The
next few poses he identified immediately. Each correct
answer seemed to add to his confidence, as she'd hoped.

This might work. She realized how uncertain she'd
been about helping him.

And how pleased she was that she could.

The clock on the wall beside the sink chimed nine
times, and Eli was astonished more than two hours had
passed since he and Kyle had arrived at the Hartz farm.

He stood. "*Danki* for taking the time with me tonight, Miriam."

"I am glad I can help. Tomorrow evening at the same
time?"

"So soon?"

"The more we work together, the quicker you will
learn."

He couldn't argue with that logic. He'd be a
dummkopf not to take advantage of her willingness
to help him become adept at reading lips. "I'll talk to
Mercy and see if Kyle can go over to their house tomorrow evening."

"Kyle needs to come, too, at the beginning. He must
learn to face you and enunciate when he speaks."

"Enough what when he speaks?"

"E-nun-ci-ate. To say something clearly."

He nodded, flustered he'd misunderstood her.

Before he could lower his head or look away, she put
one hand on either side of his face. Startled, he froze.
He hadn't expected her to be so brazen. He could sense
every inch of her skin against his as if it were his own.

A warmth coursed over his cheeks, teasing his arms to slip around her, pulling her closer.

Her words shattered the daydream. "Eli, do not be embarrassed. You missed one word I said. Even people with perfect hearing miss words."

"Not all the time like I do." He tried to shake aside the cloying image of her in his arms. He must concentrate on what she was saying.

"True, but you will learn. You will miss less then."

"You make this sound like it will solve everything."

She lowered her hands and put them on her waist in the pose of a *mamm* about to scold a *kind*. "Are you feeling sorry for yourself? Or are you trying to make me feel sorry for you?"

"Neither. I don't want pity."

"You understood everything I said."

"Because I caught enough to know what you were saying."

Not moving, she said, "And how I am standing gave you a clue, ain't so?"

"Ja." Wonder slipped into his voice. *"Ja,* it did. Is it really that easy?"

"For simple situations, *ja.* You have got a lot to learn before you can function well at a group event like when the men get together to discuss our new *Ordnung.*"

"I hope I do better at the next meeting."

"You have six days to practice what you have begun to learn." She continued to speak slow enough for him to figure out what she was saying.

If everyone would speak at that speed...

That was a futile wish. Hearing people—himself included before the accident—never thought about how fast they spoke. To expect them to change was foolish.

Instead, he needed to master the skills Miriam was willing to teach him.

"Six days isn't long," he said as he realized the enormity of the task ahead of him.

"It can be long enough to master the basics. It is up to you how you want to look at this challenge."

He reached for his straw hat he'd set on a chair behind him. "The real problem I've got is trying to follow a conversation that jumps from one person to someone else, because I can't guess who's going to be talking next. It was extra hard because I couldn't see everyone's face."

"You should have asked everyone to move so you could see."

"I didn't want to make trouble."

"What trouble would it be to move a chair?" When he didn't answer, she came around the table and put a hand on his arm. Warmth spread from where her fingers touched his skin, but her attention was on his face.

Was his pain emblazoned there? As he'd told her, the last thing he wanted was her pity.

He realized how he'd misread her when she said, "Eli, your hearing loss is nothing to be ashamed of."

"I know."

"You say that. You do not act that way. It will get easier." She smiled as if he was one of her scholars.

Was that how she saw him? As a student? That *was* what he was, but when she touched him, even with a motion as commonplace as putting her fingers on his arm to get his attention, he couldn't think of her as anything other than a charming woman.

She was his teacher! That and his neighbor. Nothing else. He was being a fool. He wasn't going to invite more pain into his life. Not when he'd come to Harmony Creek to start over.

"It will get easier," Miriam said again when he didn't answer.

"Really?"

"Really. Eli, you want this. You will learn." She smiled. "Just as Mercy is learning to speak *Deitsch*. It may be slow, but it will be worth the time you spend practicing."

"I hope you're right." He caught sight of a short silhouette near the buggy he'd left between the barn and the house. Kyle was returning. The other shadow with him must be Caleb.

Eli needed to leave, though it was tempting to stay and chat with Caleb. For too long, his only company had been Kyle. He loved the little boy, but it would be a true blessing to have the opportunity to speak with another adult. But lingering to talk with Caleb would be, he had to admit, simply an excuse to spend more time with Miriam.

"*Danki* again," he said, walking toward the door. He turned to face her. "Sorry to run like this, but I've got meetings for prospective jobs tomorrow."

"Are you taking Kyle with you? He is welcome to stay here whenever you need someone to watch him."

"That's kind of you when you've got the scholars here five days a week. I'll try to arrange to do my business during the time he's here at school, but that may not always be possible."

"Especially with *Englischers* on fast time."

He nodded. Plain families didn't set their clocks forward an hour in the spring and turn them back in the fall. That meant they had to be aware of the hour's difference in the summer when they went to an *Englisch* store or had a *doktor* appointment.

"But if Kyle is here, will you be able to get the gist of what is being discussed in your meetings?"

Trust Miriam to see beyond the facade that fooled everybody. When he looked into her gentle face, he saw honest curiosity. As if he was just like everyone else. He wondered if she knew how much of a gift that was.

"I will do my best."

"No one can ask more." A smile tugged at the corners of her lips. "Just remember. It is okay to ask someone to repeat what they said."

"*Danki*, Miriam." How many times was he going to repeat that tonight? He needed to go. Now! "I'll practice as much as I can."

"*Gut.* I will see you tomorrow when you drop Kyle off for school and tomorrow evening for your next lesson."

He put his hat on his head, but before he could leave, her fingers curved along his face as she turned his face toward hers. She lowered her fingers, but the resonance of her touch lingered on his skin as he stared at her lips. Her oh-so-kissable lips. They were moving, but instead of watching them to determine what she was saying, he imagined them against his own.

With a gulp was certain could be heard throughout the hollow, he bid her good-night and left while he still could keep himself from kissing her. If Caleb thought he was being terse as Eli collected his nephew and got into the buggy, he didn't say anything.

Eli looked back as he drove toward the twisting road.

Miriam stood in the doorway. To greet her brother or to watch the buggy leave? He didn't want to know the answer.

Chapter Seven

Eli was rising from the breakfast table in his sunny kitchen the following Tuesday morning when he saw someone at the back door. It opened, and Caleb stuck his head in.

"Busy?" he asked.

"No, *komm* in," Eli called, hoping his practice for the past week on what Miriam had been teaching him would allow him to understand what the settlement's founder had to say. He'd spent an hour with Miriam each evening and done more work after he came home. To be honest, he was tired of looking at his own mouth in the mirror, though—and again he had to be honest—he couldn't imagine getting tired of watching Miriam's.

Heat rushed through him when Caleb walked into the kitchen. To have such thoughts of his friend's sister... He hoped Caleb wasn't as aware of body language as Miriam was. Otherwise, his friend might guess how often Eli's thoughts centered on her.

"Kaffi?" he asked, hoping his voice didn't sound as raspy as it felt in his tight throat.

"Sounds *gut*." Caleb glanced at the table where Kyle

was wiping the last of the butter and syrup from his plate with a folded pancake. Turning to Eli, he said, "I hope I am not interrupting your breakfast."

Miriam must have told her brother not to use contractions so it'd be simpler for Eli to make out what he said. He appreciated Caleb's efforts, though Eli guessed it would be difficult for everyone, including Miriam, not to use them. Eli hoped soon he'd be able to read lips well enough so it wouldn't matter.

"I'm done." He grinned at his nephew, happy he'd caught enough of what Caleb had said. "Kyle eats more than I do. I don't know where he puts it."

"Into growing bigger, ain't so?" Caleb laughed.

His nephew grinned as if Caleb had given him a compliment. Eli smiled. Boys at Kyle's age started having growth spurts. Just as Eli and his brother had when…

Pain surged through him. His brother hadn't been the easiest person to get along with, because Milan had always been very sure of his opinions. On the other hand, he'd stood up for Eli whenever someone picked on him. Milan had said more than once that was how it should be. He'd claimed that older brothers had to be smarter so they could look out for their younger brothers.

But it should have gone both ways. Eli should have checked the wall in spite of Milan's reassurances it was fine. If he had, his brother and his sister-in-law would be around to watch their *kind* growing and changing from a toddler into a sprouting boy.

"…a few minutes of…time," Caleb said.

Eli pulled his attention back to the other man as he finished filling a cup with steaming *kaffi*. He needed to watch Caleb's lips to know what his friend was saying. It would be simpler if Miriam's brother spoke more slowly, but Eli was the one who needed to adjust to the "fast time" speaking of the world around him.

"Sure." He hoped Caleb had asked to speak to him. It was the obvious thing for Caleb to say upon his arrival. "Let's take our *kaffi* into the living room. That will give Kyle time to wash before I take him to school."

The boy grimaced, but his nephew loved spending time with the other *kinder* and Miriam at the temporary school. Kyle did his kitchen chores without complaint when it meant they'd soon be hitching the buggy and heading toward the Hartz farm. Any other time, his nephew made sure Eli heard and witnessed his annoyance at having to do what he called "girls' work." Eli had made the mistake—only once—of reminding his nephew they didn't have girls in the house. Kyle had suggested that could be resolved if Eli would get married.

He almost snorted at the thought. Who would want to marry a man who had lost his hearing in the accident that had claimed his brother and sister-in-law? An accident Eli should have been able to prevent. If he couldn't save his own family, how could any woman trust him?

Not wanting to become mired in self-pity, Eli led the way into the front room. His living room was simple, even by plain standards. A sofa that had seen better days and an antique rocker with a propane floor lamp were arranged on the bare floor. He'd sold their furniture except for the rocker, which his *grossdawdi* had made for *Mamm* to use to rock her *kinder*. It'd been in Milan's house, and Eli had brought it along because Kyle had sat in it for hours after Milan's and Shirley's deaths. The boy had retreated there when he was sad or upset for more than a year.

Eli had found the sofa and the battered table in the kitchen at a secondhand dealer south of Salem. He'd uncovered two beds and a desk with one leg shorter than the others in the dealer's crowded barns where everything was stored haphazardly. After cleaning the furniture, putting a new leg on the desk and painting the headboards on Kyle's bed and his own, the pieces barely resembled the ones he'd dug out of the barns.

Caleb chose the rocker, so Eli dropped onto the sofa. The thick cushion hid how the springs were almost worn out.

"What brings you by this morning?" Eli asked.

After taking a sip, Caleb made a face. He reverted to his usual smile, but Eli wasn't surprised. Miriam's *kaffi* was far superior to his own, which was why he looked forward to having a cup or two during their lessons.

"Volunteers…fire department… Chief is happy…" Caleb set his cup on the floor beside him and sat straighter so he could face Eli. Had Miriam told her brother to look at Eli while talking to him, or had Caleb gotten into the habit when visiting with his *gross-mammi*? Asking someone to look directly at him was a request, she'd reminded Eli more than once, he needed to be comfortable making. "The chief is having training on Saturday. Will you be able to attend?"

Eli grinned. He hadn't heard every word Caleb had spoken, but he'd been able to piece enough together by watching the other man's lips.

"Ja."

"The local fire department is really grateful to have

so many volunteers from the Harmony Creek settlement."

"That's no surprise." As they'd discussed before, the plain farmers—and Eli, whose work must be within ten miles so he could get there each day with the horse and buggy—would be nearby during the day. *"Ja,"* he repeated. "I'll be there on Saturday."

He focused on Caleb's lips as the other man spoke. *"Gut."* He handed Eli a piece of paper with a name and number on it. "Call him." A flush rose up Caleb's face. "Or why don't I let him know you're coming when I call with the final list of who can go?"

Eli realized anew Miriam's advice to gauge someone else's stance and expression was more important than he'd guessed. Between Caleb's ruddy cheeks and how his gaze shifted away, Eli knew the other man was embarrassed at suggesting Eli use a phone. Since the accident, the few times he'd had to make a call, he'd had Kyle listen and relay to him what was being said.

"I appreciate that, Caleb. *Danki.*" He took a drink of *kaffi* and grimaced. It hadn't improved with age since he first started it around 5:00 a.m.

"The chief is looking forward to meeting you and Jeremiah because you've got experience working with a volunteer fire department." Caleb faltered, then said, "I told him about your hearing loss, and he said your experience is more valuable to him and the department than how much you can hear."

Eli nodded, grateful to Caleb for handling the uncomfortable topic. Now he had to prove only his firefighting skills to everyone else.

"Don't worry about Kyle," Caleb went on. "I'm sure Miriam will be glad to watch him while you go to the training. She thinks a lot of him. She says he's very *gut* during school." He grinned. "Something she can't say about all the scholars. The younger Bowman boys have tried her patience every day."

Eli recalled her expression when, after that first lesson, she'd offered to watch Kyle. She'd been generous to offer, but he sensed she preferred not to have *kinder* underfoot beyond the school day. "Before I bother your sister, I'll check with Mercy. She's been asking for Kyle to come and play with her *kinder*. Let me see if she's willing to have Kyle on Saturday. If Mercy and the kids are busy, I'll ask Miriam."

"That sounds like a plan." Standing and picking up his cup, but not taking another drink, Caleb went into the kitchen. He set the cup in the sink, then reached into his pocket. "Here. Chief Pulaski asked…pager to each of our volunteers. Just…look it over and be ready with questions on Saturday."

"It beeps when there's an emergency?"

"*Ja*, and they vibrate. We…hear them over noise… machinery."

"*Gut.*"

After telling Kyle to enjoy his day at school, Caleb left to deliver the other pagers.

Eli gestured for Kyle to grab his lunch box so they could leave, too. Herding the boy out of the house, Eli took a quick glance at the kitchen clock beside the stove. He needed to run into the village and get supplies for finishing the school. He should be done with it by early July. Would Miriam be glad to get the scholars out of her makeshift schoolroom and into the new building? Most likely.

In the buggy, Kyle stared at the pager peeking out of

Eli's pocket. His nephew tapped him on the arm, and as soon as Eli looked at him, asked, "How old do I have to be before I can get one of these?"

"A few more years at least."

"After I am done with school?"

He nodded, not wanting to say no fire department was going to let a fourteen-year-old join as a volunteer. As he turned his attention to the road, keeping to the far right in case a car came past, he was grateful Kyle had heeded Miriam. The boy had gotten Eli's attention before he began talking.

When they reached the Hartz farm, Eli walked Kyle to the barn. The *kind* could have gone alone, but the chance to speak—even for a few minutes—to Miriam was too enticing to resist.

His steps slowed as he approached the barn. Miriam wore the brittle smile she did every morning when she welcomed the scholars. The *kinder* didn't seem to notice, or maybe they thought that was her normal smile.

Eli knew better. He'd seen her true smile. It glowed in her eyes and lit her face, easing the sadness hanging over her like a cloud that never dispersed. Again, he wondered what sorrow plagued her. Was it as appalling as his own?

That evening Eli and Kyle walked into the barn again. Caleb greeted them before picking up *The Budget* and walking into one of the "rooms" that had quilts for walls. He lowered the quilt serving as the door. Light from a lamp appeared around the edges along with the sound of the pages rattling as he opened the newspaper.

Eli appreciated Caleb giving them privacy for tonight's lesson. Having someone witness his stumbling attempts to grasp everything Miriam said would be embarrassing. No matter how many times she told him he shouldn't be ashamed of his disability, he couldn't shake that reaction whenever he messed up and couldn't get the gist of a conversation.

When Kyle rushed over to Miriam, chattering nonstop, Eli hung back. His nephew couldn't hide his delight at seeing his teacher again. Eli hadn't seen that big grin since… He couldn't remember the last time Kyle had been so giddy with happiness. The boy's smile broadened more when Miriam squatted so their eyes were level as she listened to whatever Kyle was saying too swiftly for Eli to catch it.

An odd sensation roiled through him. An unpleasant sensation that again felt too much like envy.

Nonsense! He couldn't be envious of his nephew, who was so comfortable with Miriam and brought out her genuine smile.

But he was.

He wanted to be the one she welcomed with joy. He longed to be able to gaze into her grass-green eyes and see a glow that was only for him.

As she came back to her feet, Eli pushed that distressing thought out of his head. He'd learned his lesson— or he should have—about how sweet smiles quickly could become pity.

Miriam took Kyle's hand, and they walked to the table. They sat and looked at him, clearly baffled about why he was hesitating to join them.

He took his seat. He should be grateful either his expression hadn't revealed his thoughts or Miriam's keen eyes hadn't noticed it while she talked with Kyle.

The lesson went as the previous ones had with her

drilling him on different words and asking him to show his progress with Kyle's help. He stumbled more than once as he attempted to keep his mind on his task.

"Watch my lips." She frowned when he failed to respond properly to what she'd said.

He was tempted to tell her he'd been doing that far too much, and that was the reason he couldn't focus. He nodded, not trusting his voice. It might give away the thoughts he shouldn't be having.

Caleb emerged, put the folded newspaper on the table and shot his sister a sympathetic glance. He announced he needed to go next door and asked Kyle if he wanted to come along to see his best friend. The boy eagerly agreed.

Eli knew Caleb's offer was a ploy to prevent any further distractions. It didn't help. Once Eli and Miriam were alone, he found his concentration wandering more. Not only did he want to watch Miriam's lips, but he also couldn't keep his gaze from admiring her pert nose and high cheekbones. He noticed for the first time a few faint freckles there.

He wondered what else he could learn about her at the same time he kept his pain hidden so he didn't have to watch her warm smile change to disgust as Betty Ann's had.

"Keep practicing," Miriam said wearily. It was obvious Eli had other matters on his mind tonight. She hoped he hadn't decided he'd learned enough. He'd made great progress, but still had a lot to learn. "Do not get discouraged. You have hit a plateau. It happens with a new skill. You will break through again soon."

"I'm sure you're right." He stood. "I should head over

to Mercy's and get Kyle." He gave her an uneven grin. "I'm glad he had a chance to play with Paul. I know you want him here so he can learn what I'm learning, but he needs time to be a *kind*."

"I agree. A youngster must have responsibilities so he or she can learn what they need to know, but they also have to have time to play and explore and learn on their own." Rising, she sighed. "If they do not get it, they may do something stupid and get themselves into trouble."

"Do you believe that?"

"Ja."

He was amazed. "Why do you look at *kinder* so negatively? I thought you liked them."

"I do, but as their teacher, I must be prepared for whatever they think up. I pray nothing bad happens. If it does, I can be of more help if I know what they might do."

"But if you look on the positive side, you can still be prepared."

"I do not know how. I know I must be ready for whatever could happen."

How could she explain to him how a little boy had nearly died because she hadn't paid enough attention? If she'd considered the many ways a little boy could get into trouble beforehand, she could have halted him from going into the pond in the first place. She wouldn't make the same mistake with Kyle, but without revealing the truth, she couldn't reassure Eli. She prayed he'd trust her as much as she wanted to trust herself.

"I guess I worry too much about the scholars," she said, glad to speak the truth.

"I don't think anyone would want it any other way,

though no *kind* wants to be smothered by too much attention. They need to have elbow room to explore and learn."

"Within limits."

"I agree. As Kyle's *onkel*, I have a duty to him as you do for the scholars."

She came around the table. "Before you go, I need to ask you one thing. Kyle asked me today if I would talk to you about him staying after school to play ball with the other boys."

"No."

She was shocked by his terse answer. After his comments about how she was being too protective of the *kinder*—smothering was the word he'd used—he was acting that way himself.

Eli reached for his straw hat. "It's my duty to rear my brother's *kind*. I don't take that lightly. As soon as school is out, Kyle needs to come to the schoolhouse where I can keep an eye on him. I'm sure you understand."

She didn't, but she should be grateful she'd be watching out for one less *kind*. Yet, when she thought about the disappointment on the little boy's face each time he couldn't stay and play ball with the others, she understood how important it was for Kyle to feel like he was a part of the community of the settlement's *kinder*.

However, Kyle needed to obey the rules Eli set. Having those rules was a parent's duty. To keep a *kind* safe and out of trouble as well as teaching the skills a youngster would need to be a vital part of the community when he or she became an adult.

"I will send him across the road after our lessons are done," she said before she half turned so she didn't have to look at him as she spoke the unpleasant words.

"You think I'm wrong."

"It is not my place to say whether you are right or wrong."

When his broad hand settled on her shoulder, she almost jumped out of her skin. She hadn't thought he'd touch her when they stood in the barn's doorway. If someone happened to see...

Bringing her to face him, he said, "I can't read your lips if you're not looking at me."

"I am sorry." She was, because she'd forgotten the very first lesson she'd taught him and Kyle.

"What did you say when you were turned away?"

"That I should not judge what you are doing. Kyle is your nephew, and you know what he needs better than anyone."

Grief swept across his face, but vanished as fast as it'd appeared. "*Danki*, Miriam. I'll see you tomorrow."

"You will?" A silly question, because he always dropped Kyle off for school before heading across the road. She was letting herself become bemused by his brilliant blue eyes and curiosity about what thoughts were hidden behind them. That was foolish. Hadn't she—seconds ago—been irritated by how curt he'd been while dismissing her request on his nephew's behalf? And now she was losing herself in a fantasy of spending time with him.

She wasn't a teenage girl, waiting for the boy she had her eye on to ask to take her home after a singing.

She was far wiser than that young girl, or so she'd believed. Now she wasn't so sure.

Eli wasn't a callow young man who looked at the world with eager eyes. He'd suffered too much of a loss.

As he bid her good-night and walked out to collect

his nephew, she blinked back tears. She was sad for Eli and herself and all they'd lost.

And all they could never have together.

Chapter Eight

Laughter sounded outside the barn as Miriam was drying the last dish from Saturday's midday meal. Not just any laughter, but Annie Wagler's distinctive laugh that was impossible not to join in with.

Wearing a broad smile, Miriam went to the door and greeted the other members of the Harmony Creek Spinsters' Club who were carrying cardboard boxes. She was delighted to see Sarah with the twins. The redhead must have the day off from working as a nanny.

With the sun shining, the June day wasn't too hot. Bees swarmed through the shrubs, looking for flowers they hadn't visited. In the distance she could hear the lowing of cows and a soft tinkling sound.

"Hear that?" asked Annie.

"It sounds like a bell." Miriam stepped aside to let her friends into the barn.

"From Leanna's new goats." Annie smiled at her twin. "She plans to make goat milk soap *and* goat milk cheese to sell at the Salem farmers market later this summer."

"You're going to be busy." Miriam chuckled. "Or busier."

Leanna wagged a finger at her. "Look who's talking. We've heard Caleb finished your kitchen, and it was the final room he had to do before you could move in."

"Not quite. The upstairs needs to be painted."

"So you're using both floors?" asked Sarah.

"No. Not right now."

"Then the house is done." Annie's tone dared anyone to disagree with her. "Done enough for us to help you move your things from here to the house."

"Now?"

"Do you know a better time?" Leanna dimpled. "You don't have to teach today, and Caleb is at the firefighter training with the other men. We can take your household items over and have them put away in the cupboards before the men bring in the furniture."

Sarah added, "You do so much for others, Miriam. Let us do this for you."

"Because we're going to anyhow." Annie's laughter drew everyone into her *gut* spirits.

Miriam didn't answer, because she realized whatever she said wouldn't have made any difference. Her friends had decided upon the perfect frolic for a quiet Saturday, and she was grateful for their help with a chore she hadn't been looking forward to.

No one was surprised when Annie gave each of them instructions for their tasks. She worked as hard as the rest of them did, maybe harder, because she toted many of the heavier boxes they packed to the house herself.

Miriam began to unpack in the kitchen and admired its soft tan walls. Caleb had added new cupboards to the ones he'd been able to salvage from the original kitchen. Once he'd painted them white, they looked as if they'd always been hung together. The propane refrigerator was a generous size, but the centerpiece of the kitchen was Caleb's double wide stove with its massive ovens. He had plans for using it, though he hadn't shared them with her yet.

By four, they had moved about half of the portable items from the barn to the house. Miriam grinned as she served her friends lemonade from a pitcher stored in the new refrigerator. She led the way out to the porch. Sitting on the steps because the chairs remained in the barn, she scanned the horizon.

Mountains rose to the north, west and east. To the south, the river valley was edged with distant hills. Caleb had been excited when he found farms for sale edging the north side of Harmony Creek, and now that she lived here, she understood why.

"Pretty, isn't it?" Sarah asked nobody in particular.

Miriam smiled. "Caleb says when the leaves start turning in the fall, it's as if someone melted a box of red, orange and yellow crayons along the hillsides."

Sipping her lemonade, she took a deep breath and glanced at the road where a silver car drove past at a reasonable pace. She recognized it as belonging to the farm next to the Kuhnses'. When the driver waved out the open window, Miriam waved back.

"He's not there, you know," Sarah murmured.

"He?" repeated Miriam, wondering what she'd missed.

"Eli." Before Miriam could ask what her friend meant, Sarah went on, "We've noticed how you avoid looking at the schoolhouse. I thought you were helping Eli make sure everything is in the proper place."

Miriam tried not to flinch as Sarah patted her shoulder in silent commiseration before putting down her empty glass and heading back toward the barn for another box. She *had* been using any excuse to keep from checking the school's progress. Since her last conversation with Eli, when he had refused to let Kyle join the other scholars for an after-school softball game, she hadn't spoken to him. He seemed to agree, because he hadn't come back for lipreading lessons.

She was sure it was for the best. When they'd been alone the other night, she'd lost herself in imagining what it would be like to be in Eli's arms. She'd been shown how dangerous for her equilibrium it could be to spend time with him.

Caleb had asked what was wrong and why she wasn't working with Eli any longer. She'd given him a shrug because she wasn't sure. Maybe Eli believed he didn't need further lessons. He'd caught on quickly, but there was more she could teach him. Things like refining his skills so he was more comfortable with a group of people.

"I'm supposed to help him if he's got questions," Miriam said, realizing her friends were waiting for an answer. "And I do, when he's there. He's at the training session today with Caleb and the other men."

"He's going to be a firefighter?" asked Annie, her eyes wide.

Miriam nodded. "Caleb tells me that Eli is an experienced firefighter. He volunteered in Delaware."

"Surely that was before he lost his hearing."

Leanna frowned at her sister. "Annie, you don't know anything about being a firefighter. It's something Eli must be able to do, or he wouldn't be attending the training today."

"I'm sorry. I shouldn't have said that, but I'm surprised he can work with the others without being able to hear them." She rushed to catch up with Sarah, who was at the barn.

"Forgive her," Leanna said. "She speaks before she thinks." Chuckling, she added, "And I think too much, and I don't speak before the conversation has moved on."

"It's already forgotten," Miriam reassured her friend. "Annie asks so many questions because she cares about everyone and everything. And to tell you the truth, there have been a bunch of times that I've been glad that she's asked questions I wanted to know the answer to."

"Me, too."

Miriam thought that would be the end of the uncomfortable subject of her spending time with Eli, but as her friends were about to leave, Leanna took her aside and apologized again for her sister's comments.

"Don't worry," Miriam said. "I've forgotten about it." *Just as I wish you three would forget about there being anything between Eli and me. He's made it clear he doesn't want that.*

"I'm glad." She glanced at the nearly finished schoolhouse. "And I'm glad you're helping Eli with the school. It'll make teaching much easier for the next teacher."

"Like I said, I offer help when he asks. Otherwise, I don't want to get in Eli's way. He doesn't need an audience when he's working. If he gets distracted, he could get injured."

Leanna's smile turned soft. "You do care about him."

"Don't read any extra meaning into my words."

"I don't have to. Your expression says it all." She hugged Miriam before her twin came toward them with Sarah not far behind.

Not wanting the conversation to turn to Eli again, Miriam said as the four of them walked back into the house and into the kitchen, "*Danki* for helping today."

"It was fun," Annie said. "We'd like to have another frolic, if we could. Can we join you while you're teaching school one of these days?"

"You want to help me with the scholars?"

"Ja." She smiled. "It'd give us a chance to get to know the *kinder* better. These kids are like we were when we thought that being with an adult was boring."

"You're blessed to be able to spend so much time with the girls and boys." Leanna glanced around the kitchen and sighed. "It's like having a huge family of your own."

"A family who goes home at the end of the day so I only have to cook for Caleb and me," Miriam joked to keep a wall between her heart and the anguish of losing her chance to have the family she'd loved. When a pulse of pain didn't thud through her, she was astonished.

Maybe it was because she was having fun with her friends, and the grief that had been her unfailing companion for months was beginning to dull. Would it stay like that? If someone had asked her before, she would have denied her anguish would diminish.

Whatever the reason, she was grateful for the temporary reprieve.

"Ach," sighed Leanna. "I wouldn't mind if I had two dozen to cook for each day if I could have a family of my own."

Annie watched her twin walk out of the kitchen. For

once, Annie wasn't smiling. As if to herself, she said, "I wish Leanna wouldn't obsess about getting married. I'm afraid she's going to become so desperate to get wed that she'll agree to any proposal that comes her way."

"Even if it's not Caleb asking?"

"Caleb?" Annie's eyes grew big.

"I saw how Leanna looked at him the nights we've met to discuss the rules for our new *Ordnung*. She seems taken with him."

For a long minute Annie said nothing, and Miriam could tell her friend was taken aback. How could Annie have failed to notice how her sister had reacted each time Caleb spoke, whether he was in the midst of the debate about buggies or the use of solar panels?

"I guess I was paying too much attention to the discussion," Annie replied at last. "I've been praying she doesn't do something stupid like ask someone to marry her without waiting for him to ask."

"Why do you think she'd do that? Leanna is sensible. Why wouldn't she wait for the man to ask her?"

"She tried that before, and he asked someone else."

"I'm sorry to hear that. She must have been heart-broken."

"She was because she hadn't realized he was walking out with the other girl while bringing Leanna home from singings." Annie's mouth tightened. "I tell her that any man who does such a thing doesn't deserve her, but she believes the only thing that will mend her heart is getting married herself."

"That's so sad."

"I know." She drew in a deep breath and then sighed. "I keep praying she'll find someone to marry for love not for revenge."

"I'll pray for her, too. A marriage based on vengeance can't be happy."

"*Danki*, Miriam." She squeezed Miriam's hand before heading toward the door. As she was about to leave, she paused and turned. "Please don't think Leanna is foolish."

"I'd never think that."

"She needs to prove to herself that she's worthy of being loved."

"All she has to do is open her eyes and look at her twin."

Annie smiled faintly. "She wants more than a sister's love."

"But she's blessed to have you worried about her."

"And I'm blessed to have her." Annie started to add more, but halted when Sarah called her name.

Miriam waved goodbye before opening one of the last boxes they'd toted from the barn. She put the pots and pans in the lower cupboards to the right of the big stove. On the left, she planned to store baking pans and casserole dishes.

Her eyes were caught by a motion beyond the window over the double sink. Two little boys raced out of the woods. Her heart swelled as she thought about Ralph and his buddies, but reality hit. It wasn't Ralph, the boy she'd loved almost as much as his *daed*.

Maybe more, she admitted.

Again, she was disconcerted by her own thoughts. Could that be true? Could she be more like Leanna than she'd guessed? Wanting a family so much she'd been willing to marry a man who could provide her with one…even if she didn't love him as much as she did his *kind*?

As she opened the door, she smiled at the two boys loping toward her.

"Kyle! Paul! Does Mercy know you are over here?"

Both boys nodded before Kyle said, "You're moving into the house, ain't so? Can we help you carry stuff?"

"The more hands, the better." Crooking a finger toward them, she said, "*Komm* with me. I'll show you which boxes you can bring over to the house."

In the barn, she selected boxes that were light enough for the boys to heft without hurting themselves. Setting them together, she said, "If you can take these to the house, it'll be a huge help."

As if it was the best game ever invented, the boys carried the boxes to the house. Miriam rewarded them with icy glasses of lemonade, which they swallowed in one gulp. She refilled the glasses, and the boys drank more slowly.

They handed her the empty glasses and bid her goodbye. Paul rushed out the door, and she smiled. It would appear the boy had one speed—fast.

Kyle paused in the doorway. "Will you talk to *Onkel* Eli again about me playing ball after school?" Before she could answer, he hurried to add, "He lets me hang out with Paul, so why won't he let me play with him and the other boys after school?"

"I don't know."

"Didn't you ask him?"

"I did, but he just said that he wanted you to come over to the school as soon as we're done with lessons. You should ask your *onkel* why he feels that way. Maybe he'll explain his reasons to you." *Though I don't know why he wouldn't tell me.*

"Will you ask him again for me?"

She wanted to say no, but the entreaty on Kyle's face halted her. "Let me think about it." It wasn't a promise or a direct no. She hoped it would be enough for the boy.

It was. He grinned and skipped out, heading toward Mercy's farm.

She closed the door and leaned against it. Raising her gaze upward, she said, "God, You keep putting Eli in my path. I know You must have a reason, and I wish You'd share it with me."

Eli looked across the table at Miriam the following Tuesday evening and sighed. Tonight's lesson, his first in the house instead of the barn, hadn't progressed as he'd hoped. It'd been over a week since his previous lesson, and he could see that she was wondering if he had practiced at all during that time. He considered telling her how much he'd comprehended during the firefighter training, but bragging about that would border on *hochmut*.

Kyle sat in the living room, looking at a picture book about farm animals. More than once, he'd glanced into the kitchen. He'd come into the kitchen only when Miriam offered him a piece of cake, the first one baked in the new oven. As soon as he was finished, he'd gone back to his book.

The boy had been on edge all day, though he hadn't said why. Eli was curious what was on his nephew's mind, but he didn't press the *kind* to explain. Kyle's *daed* had become introspective at times, and nothing Eli had done would convince Milan to talk one second sooner about what was bothering him. Maybe Kyle was the same.

"I understand you are frustrated," Miriam said.

"You've got no idea how much."

"*Ja*, I do. Remember I learned lipreading because my *grossmammi* needed help. I know it is not easy. Eventually, you will be able to read lips almost as easily as you once heard words. I am sure of that."

When she stood, he did the same, knowing it was the signal that the lesson was over. He should've looked away, but he couldn't pull his gaze from her graceful steps and the gentle sway of her dark purple hem as she went to the sink to put their cups in to soak.

He bid her a good-night and left with Kyle and the book Miriam told him he could borrow. Eli wanted to let her faith in him sustain him until he made another breakthrough. Maybe he should have told her about how he didn't have to remind himself with every encounter to be aware of body language. It was becoming almost second nature to him.

Why could he function well with everyone else but stumbled during his lessons with Miriam?

The question kept Eli awake too long and followed him to the new school the next morning after he dropped Kyle at Miriam's house for the boy's own lessons.

He had to stop during the day when yawn after yawn interrupted his work. He needed to concentrate twice as much as usual to make sure the moldings around the windows—including the extras Miriam had insisted on—were straight. Measuring multiple times, he pulled off two pieces and realigned them so they were level.

By the time Kyle arrived midafternoon, Eli felt as if he'd worked a full week, though he'd accomplished less than half of what he'd planned. His exhaustion didn't prevent him from noticing how the little boy shuffled into the school as if on his way to be punished.

"Did you have a *gut* day at school?" Eli asked.

The *kind* nodded, but didn't look up.

"What did you study today?"

He shrugged.

"Kyle, look at me."

His nephew regarded him with tear-filled eyes.

Before Eli could ask what was wrong, the crack of a bat and cheers came from the other side of the road. The scholars were playing a game of softball before heading home to help with evening chores. Every instinct urged him to relent, but how could he work at the schoolhouse when his nephew was out of his sight? Going to school was one thing. The state required it, and Eli didn't want to get their new settlement in trouble with the authorities. As well, Kyle was being watched by Miriam. She wouldn't be able to oversee the *kinder* as closely while she finished her daily household tasks and made supper for her brother.

Kyle sighed.

"I was honest with your teacher. I need your help here." Was Eli trying to convince himself or the boy the half lie was the whole truth?

"I know." The *kind*'s head was down, and he scuffled his feet across the floor, every step broadcasting how angry he was at being thwarted from joining his friends for the game.

When Eli suggested Kyle play with the marbles they'd picked up in Salem on their last visit, the boy acted as if he hadn't heard. Eli took his nail gun and moved to the molding for the back door beyond where the teacher's desk would be placed. He tried to work, but the quiet in the building was appalling, even for a man whose world was blanketed in silence.

He turned to see Kyle standing by a window Eli had finished. His nephew stared out, hunger on his young face. Eli knew the little boy was watching the *kinder* in Caleb's yard. The sharp sound of another ball against a bat exploded, and Kyle stood on tiptoe to watch the batter run the bases as the other team scrambled to stop the ball and throw it in to prevent the home run.

Eli sighed. Miriam had been right about the importance of body language when he couldn't see someone's face. Just by observation, he could tell what someone else was saying.

And what they weren't saying.

Kyle's muteness spoke more clearly than the little boy could. He didn't want to play marbles all alone. He wanted to play with the other *kinder*, to be part of something bigger than himself.

Instead of protecting his nephew, Eli was breaking his heart by keeping him from doing what the rest of the *kinder* could. That wouldn't have been what his brother would have wanted.

It was time to admit he'd made a mistake.

"I'll be right back, Kyle," he said, disconnecting his nail gun from the air compressor and setting it on the floor.

Either the boy didn't answer or Eli didn't hear him.

Crossing the road, he edged around the improvised ball field where a new batter was getting ready to swing. He headed toward the house. He opened the door and called Miriam's name.

"Eli!" She walked into the kitchen from the living room. Her blond hair was covered by a black kerchief, and she held a wet rag. A bucket on the floor by the front windows showed that she was washing them. "Are we supposed to have a lesson this afternoon?"

"No."

"Are you looking for Caleb, then?"

He shook his head as he closed the distance between them. "No." His eyes took in the splatters of water that created small dark circles on her dark green dress. A single strand of blond hair had slipped from her bun and hung draped over her right ear. Soapsuds curved along her cheek where she must have pushed her hair back. His fingers itched to follow the same path across her face, caressing her soft skin.

To keep from giving in to the impulse, he said, "I want to talk to you about Kyle."

Miriam dropped the wet cloth in the sink and faced Eli. "That is *gut* because I want to talk to you about him, too. I realize I have asked you about letting Kyle stay after school to play ball with the other *kinder* and you have given me your answer."

"*Ja*, but—"

"But you are wrong, Eli! That boy needs to spend time with his school friends."

"I know, and—"

Again, she interrupted with, "It is important for a *kind* to learn more than what is in books. He needs to discover about what it means to be part of a team. That teaches him the importance of community and how we must depend on each other as well as upon God."

"Miriam—"

"Let me say what I've got to say, and then I'll listen to what you have to say. Kyle has become more droopy each day. You must have noticed, too."

"I have."

"You're too overprotective." She realized she was using contractions, but couldn't halt herself as her tone became heated. He wouldn't hear that. She folded her arms in front of her and narrowed her eyes, wanting him to understand her fervor as she spoke on his nephew's behalf. "I know you want to keep Kyle safe. Every adult wants that for *kinder*, but one thing I have learned is if you don't give a *kind* a bit of freedom, he or she will take it anyhow and get into much bigger trouble."

She had to struggle to get the last few words out. Yost had vacillated between being too protective and too indifferent to his son. At first when she began walking out with Yost, he'd insisted upon knowing where the boy was every minute of the day. Later, he had handed that duty over to her and berated her when she didn't smother Ralph as he had. His final words to her, after Ralph's near-drowning, had been a furious, "I told you so."

She didn't want Eli to make the same mistake. Though the two men were different in many ways, if Eli continued to stifle Kyle's natural exuberance, his nephew was going to act as thoughtlessly as Ralph had.

Eli cleared his throat. "I should tell you before you go any further, what I wanted to talk to you about."

She lowered her eyes. Were Annie's outspoken ways rubbing off on her?

"I wanted to tell you," he went on, "that I've changed my mind. If you'll assure me that you'll keep a close eye on the *kinder* while they're in your yard, I'm willing to let Kyle join the games after school."

Shock blocked every word she could think of. Finally, as he began to smile, she asked, "Why didn't you say so right from the beginning?"

"You didn't give me a chance."

"True." Her cheeks grew warm. "I am sorry about that."

He chuckled, and his eyes lit with *gut* humor. It was an expression she savored each time he smiled. "No need to be sorry. You couldn't have guessed I was willing to change my mind. Let's try it for next week and see what happens."

"Just a week? Okay." She laughed when his mouth dropped open. "Did you think I would not agree?"

"You've got as much work as the rest of us, and you've taken on teaching the scholars."

"Someone had to."

"But nobody else did except you. Are you always this willing to put aside what you need and want for others?"

"I try to be now."

"Now? Did something happen before?"

Miriam berated herself. How could she make such an obvious reference to the past when Eli was making it clear he was letting Kyle stay after school because he trusted her with his nephew? If he knew the truth…

No, that must never happen.

Chapter Nine

"Let's go to the Fourth of July parade and carnival in Salem together!" Annie's eyes sparkled as she cut tops off the strawberries she and Leanna had picked that morning at a nearby farm. They'd come home with enough berries for each member of the Spinsters' Club to make shortcake for supper.

"It's supposed to be a fun, family-oriented celebration," her twin added.

"And the money raised at the carnival benefits the fire department."

"Having a *gut* time and helping the firefighters. What could be better?"

"Did you hear there's going to be an auction? A cake auction!"

"We spinsters will have to donate cakes, ain't so?"
"Ja!"

Miriam grinned as the twins continued talking at the same time. Neither she nor Sarah attempted to interject a word. Not that they had a chance. Somehow, each twin seemed to understand everything the other said, even when their words bounced off one another as they did while they made and discarded plans so quickly Miriam couldn't keep up.

"It must be a twin skill," she whispered to Sarah after she went to check—again—on the scholars who would soon be finishing their after-school ball game.

"They say one twin always knows what the other is thinking." Her grin revealed her dimples. "It must be true. Otherwise, they'd be as confused as we are."

Annie broke off the conversation with her sister to ask, "What are you two talking about?"

"We could ask you the same thing," Miriam said.

The twins shared a bewildered glance before Leanna replied in a tone that suggested she had no idea why they would have to ask, "We're talking about our next Spinsters' Club outing. We want to go to Salem for the Fourth of July celebrations. Let's go together! What do you say?"

"I can go," Miriam said, cutting more of the big berries into pieces and putting them in a bowl. Her fingers and the knife were stained with the luscious-smelling juice, and her mouth watered at the thought of having the berries for dessert later.

"Me, too." Sarah reached into one of the plastic buckets for another handful of berries.

"You don't have to work on the Fourth?"

"Just in the morning to get the *kinder* their breakfast. Both parents are home for the week, so they don't need me to stay after lunch." She smiled. "My brothers are looking forward to me making an extra cake for them while I bake one for the auction, but it won't take long."

"The parade starts around 6:00 p.m." Annie grinned. "Let's hire Hank's van to take us in and find a great place to watch the parade. Then we can go to the carnival. The dessert auction is scheduled for around eight o'clock."

"Exactly when everyone realizes they missed dessert before the parade." Miriam laughed. "That's the perfect time. The firefighters should make a lot of money by having cakes and other goodies to bid on."

She sidled once more to the window and looked at where the boys and girls were done playing for the afternoon and had stored the equipment in a wooden box by the barn door. As they began to head for home, she returned to cutting strawberries.

"Eli changed his mind about letting Kyle play, I see." Sarah wiped bright red juice off her cutting board before it could stain the counter.

"He's trying to be a *gut daed* to the boy, and he saw how much Kyle wanted to play." She didn't say how she and Eli had debated the topic multiple times before he acquiesced. Nor did she mention how nervous she was with having to keep an eye on the *kinder*.

As long as the scholars played where she could see them, she let them choose whichever games they wanted. A couple of the older boys had started to slip away, and she'd insisted they stay with the other *kinder* or go home and not play after school for the rest of the term. She guessed their plans had been no more mischievous than exploring the woods behind the barn, but she refused to relent. Kyle's probation week—as well as her own—was almost over, and everything had gone well.

"It's settled, then? We're going together to Salem?" Leanna stacked the empty buckets together to take home.

Everyone agreed enthusiastically as they divided the strawberries, and Miriam found her smile wouldn't budge from her face. Spending time with her friends would be relaxing and fun. Just what she needed while she prayed Eli would let his nephew continue to participate in the ball games for the last week and a half of school.

With his tool belt slung over his shoulder, Eli walked from the schoolhouse to the other side of the road where Kyle sat beneath a tree. Eli had asked his nephew to wait there each day, because Eli hoped there would be a chance to talk with Miriam.

Hearing female laughter coming from farther along the road, he saw the Wagler twins and Sarah Kuhns walking toward their families' farms. Had they been at Miriam's? If she had company, would she have remembered to keep a close eye on the *kinder*?

Kyle must have guessed his thoughts. "Don't worry. Miriam checked on us every few minutes like she said she would."

"That's *gut* to know."

Whatever he'd planned to say next melted away in his mind as he saw Miriam walking toward them. He'd never seen another woman who could make everyday steps appear as if she were floating on a cloud. There was a lightness about her that drew him to her, but that cloud could become stormy without warning. More than once, he'd considered asking her what darkness from her past clung to her.

He hadn't. Asking her to reveal the truth opened himself to speaking of the tragedy that shadowed his and Kyle's lives.

"How is the work going at the school?" she asked.

Curious what was in the covered plastic bowl she carried, he said, "I'm hoping you and the *kinder* can move in after the holiday. That way you'll be able to give it what the *Englischers* call a beta test before school begins in September."

"A beta test? Isn't it something to do with computers?"

"I think so, but what I mean is if you find any problems with the building, I'll have time to correct them."

That faint cloud misted across her face. "You haven't found other work yet?"

"It'll come. I trust God has a plan for me." Wanting to bring back her smile, he said, "And speaking of plans, have you thought about attending the carnival on the Fourth of July?"

"I'm going with my friends. We decided this afternoon to go together."

"Then I'll see you there."

"*Gut.* Caleb tells me the parade attracts a lot of spectators, but the route along Main Street and to the carnival grounds is long enough so there are plenty of places to watch it."

"That's what I've been told, too."

Her smile again became as bright as the sunshine. "You're doing much better with your lipreading and comprehension."

"I've had a *gut* teacher." He was pleased when her cheeks turned a deeper rose and her eyes glowed. "You've made a difference in my life. A big difference. I should have thanked you before."

"You don't need to thank me."

"I know, but I'm grateful how much easier my day-to-day life has become. There are still a lot of things I miss when I can't see someone's lips. However, I'm learning there's no shame in asking the person to repeat what was said."

"Gut." She held out the bowl. "The Wagler twins picked strawberries this morning and shared them with us. There are more than Caleb and I can eat. Would you like them?"

Kyle cheered his excitement before Eli could reply and held his hands out for the plastic bowl.

Eli put out his arm to block her from giving the strawberries to his nephew. "We've got to run into Salem. Can we pick them up later?"

"Of course. They'll be waiting for you."

He wanted to ask if she would be waiting for him, too, but halted the words before they could form. Instead, he said, "Let's go, Kyle."

"Can Miriam come with us?" He kept his face turned toward Eli, a sign Kyle didn't want a single word he spoke missed.

"Do you want to drive into Salem with us?" Eli asked.

Seeing her astonishment, he wondered if asking her to ride in his buggy had been too blunt. Not that the invitation could be construed as romantic when they would be accompanied by a six-year-old.

He was so sure she'd refuse, it was his turn to be shocked when she said,

"I need to get mayonnaise. We're out. Let me put your strawberries in the house, then I'll meet you at the school."

"That sounds *gut.*"

As Eli walked toward the school with Kyle, he admitted having time with Miriam should be far more than *gut.* He glanced at his grinning nephew. The boy was as happy as Eli was to have Miriam join them for the drive into the village.

Or was the boy giddy about something else? Like matchmaking?

Eli shook those questions out of his head. He was being ridiculous. Kyle was focused on his friends, school and softball.

Making sure no sign of his errant thoughts were on his face, he had the buggy ready by the time Miriam came across the road with a black bonnet covering her *kapp*. As soon as they were settled inside the buggy, Miriam sitting on Kyle's far side so Eli could see them at the same time, they headed toward the village.

Not that Eli or Miriam had a chance to talk while Kyle gave them a play-by-play recap of the ball game. When Miriam mentioned one of the long hits before the boy could, Eli realized Kyle was right. She was watching the *kinder* closely.

They were driving into the village, past old farmhouses and Victorian houses, before Kyle was finished. The traffic was light, so Eli held the reins loosely. He trusted Slim to go along the road without much supervision because they'd traveled that way enough times for the horse to know the way.

He glanced at Miriam. "I can drop you off at the grocery store before I do my errands, if you'd like."

"I…"

He couldn't catch the rest of her words. "Your bonnet is shading your face."

She untied her bonnet and placed it in her lap. "Is this better?"

"*Ja*. It seems I've still got a lot to learn."

"If you can't see someone's mouth to watch their lips form words, you can't read them. It's as simple as that."

"I guess it's always going to be a challenge."

"It will be," she said, "but how we face challenges reveals who we truly are. If we've got faith that God has a reason for putting those roadblocks in our way, then we can't help but realize each lesson we learn is one He wants us to discover."

As they passed the brick central school set on lush green lawns, Eli had to pay more attention to the traffic. A milk tanker rumbled past, but Slim didn't pay any more attention to it than the smaller cars. *Kinder* stopped playing and pointed as the buggy drove by. When Kyle waved to them, the youngsters couldn't hide their envy at him riding in it.

"I can get out here," Miriam said when they stopped for the red light at the intersection of Main Street and Broadway in the village. "Where do you want to meet?"

"I'll meet you in the parking lot at the grocery store in half an hour. Okay?"

"Ja." She climbed out of the buggy and crossed to the sidewalk.

Eli heard Kyle sigh beside him as Miriam strode along the street, her bonnet again in place.

"I like her," his nephew said. "A lot."

"I know."

"Do you like her, *Onkel* Eli?"

"Of course. She's our neighbor."

"And our teacher."

"True." Eli gave Slim the command to move when the light turned green.

"Do you like her a lot, too?"

He wouldn't lie to his nephew, but knew how *kinder* talked among themselves. He didn't want his name or Miriam's to be fodder for speculation.

"Kyle, look at the gas station and see if there's a place we can pull in next to one of the pumps."

As Eli had hoped, the request diverted the boy, who scanned the busy gas station on the opposite corner. Kyle pointed to an open pump in the center of the three rows.

Curious—and shocked—glances came in their direction when Eli stopped Slim by a gas pump. As he climbed out of the buggy, the man pumping gas on the other side stared so hard it looked as if his eyes were in danger of searing their imprint into the side of the buggy. Conversations faded to silence as Eli walked around the buggy and opened the back. He felt each look aimed at him, but he pretended he didn't notice as he took out two plastic gas containers.

He checked the pump and saw he could pay after he got the ten gallons the red containers could hold. Setting the pump to regular, he opened the containers. He stuck the nozzle into the first one and listened to the gas splash into it. Once he'd filled it, he repeated the process with the second container.

"I didn't think you Amish used gas," said the man on the other side of the pump, who drove a bright silver truck. A little girl, who couldn't be more than four, had her head stuck out the window and she was staring at Eli, Kyle, the buggy and Slim.

"I need it for the air compressor that runs my power tools." He put the nozzle into place and screwed the lids onto the containers. "It won't run on oats like my vehicle does."

The man grinned, then laughed as Eli hefted the containers into the buggy. "That's a good one. I wasn't sure Amish made jokes. You always look so serious."

"We make jokes, sometimes really bad ones."

That brought more laughter, and the little girl asked if she could pet Slim. After checking with the man who was probably her *daed*, Eli nodded. She squeezed past the pump. Eli halted her from running right at the horse.

"Horses don't like to be surprised," he said.

Lifting her, he let her pat the horse's nose. Slim, who was accustomed to Kyle and other *kinder*, accepted the attention as his rightful due. The little girl giggled with delight as Eli handed her to her *daed*, who thanked him.

Eli left Kyle with instructions to move the buggy if a car was waiting for gas, then went inside to pay. The store was cramped and filled with every kind of soft drink and candy bar Eli had ever seen. He ignored the treats as he thought of the fresh strawberries he and his nephew could enjoy tonight. Giving several bills to the cashier, he waited for his change.

"I thought I was seeing things," the older man said as he opened the register. "A horse and buggy in the gas station? I wouldn't have believed it if I hadn't seen it with my own two eyes." Handing Eli several coins, he added, "That's a nice-looking family you have. Saw you by the light before you came over here."

Eli was puzzled. He hadn't imagined anyone describing his nephew that way. Then he realized the man assumed Miriam was Eli's wife.

He hurried out of the gas station, but he couldn't move fast enough to get ahead of his thoughts.

Nice-looking family you have.

A family? Of his own?

After assuming responsibility for Kyle, he hadn't thought of building a family beyond the two of them. At least, not until he met Miriam Hartz. The warmth in her eyes when she looked at him suggested she might have feelings for him beyond being his teacher. Even when that gentle heat became a vexed flame, there was a softness in the way she treated him and Kyle.

"Where to next?" Kyle asked.

"The hardware store. I need to get a gallon of blackboard paint."

His nephew wrinkled his nose at the thought of lessons being put on the blackboard in the fall.

Eli chuckled and drove the buggy onto Main Street. He parked it about halfway along the street near a thin tree between the road and the sidewalk. He could trust Slim to stay without being tied, but there was more traffic along Main Street than the horse was accustomed to. He lashed the reins around the tree as Kyle jumped out and peered into the alley where grass grew in the middle, showing it wasn't used much. Together they walked up the three steps to Rossi's Hardware's front door.

Opening the door, Eli led the way into the shadowed interior. Instantly, he was transported to Kent County and the small shops where he used to buy supplies for the farm with his *daed* and brother. Those stores had displayed wares on every available surface, too.

He wasn't surprised when the worn floorboards, wider than any a modern sawmill could cut, creaked. Made dim with the dust left by hundreds of footsteps before his, they rippled like some great creature had dragged its claws along them.

Kyle wandered away to look at the tools and parts held in wooden barrels and on shelves and pegboards. A few glass cases were scattered among the stacks of rubber boots and fishing poles and other equipment.

The paint was at the rear of the store, so Eli headed that way. Using blackboard paint instead of slate saved money and time, though slate was quarried only twenty miles to the north and east. Maybe the settlement would decide on a slate chalkboard later, but for now he'd paint one behind the teacher's desk.

Finding what he needed, he carried it to a long wooden counter that must have been in the store since the business opened. He set it by the register and nodded to the heavyset man there. The man with a full head of bright white hair was Tuck Rossi, the store's proprietor.

"Did you find what you want?" Tuck asked in his booming voice.

"I did."

Tuck rang up the paint. "Is this for the school you're building in the hollow?"

"*Ja.* I mean, yes."

"You're the carpenter?"

Eli nodded as he paid for the paint.

"Do you make furniture?"

Or at least that was what Eli guessed Tuck had asked. The man talked fast, faster than most of the plain folks. But Eli seemed to be getting most of what the hardware store owner was saying. Not once had Tuck given him that peculiar glance that warned Eli that he'd made a complete mess of "translating" what someone else said.

"No, I do rough and finish carpentry, but I've got a neighbor who builds furniture. I can give you his name, if you're interested."

"*Onkel* Eli makes cabinets for kitchens and bathrooms, too," Kyle said with a grin as he came to stand by the counter.

"That's good to know." Tuck pulled a pad of paper from under the counter. "Write your contact information there. Your neighbor's, too, if you don't mind."

Eli did, wondering if he should have contacted the hardware store earlier to let folks know he was looking for work.

Tuck took the pad, glanced at it and nodded. "This is good. Some people around here don't want to drive almost an hour to Glens Falls to order cabinets. Once they find out you're around and willing to work on kitchens, you'll have more jobs than you can handle."

Thanking Tuck, Eli took Kyle's hand. They put the paint in the buggy.

Miriam hurried along the sidewalk toward them. She swung a bag by her side, and she smiled as she neared.

What would it be like to have a beautiful, kind-hearted woman like her for his own? A lovely wife and precious *kinder*, a true part of his life, not a dream he barely dared to have any longer.

Pain slashed him. That happiness had been almost within his grasp before his mistake—whatever it had been—had caused a wall to collapse and crush his hopes. He'd been careless once, and he didn't trust himself not to make the same horrific error again, no matter how hard he tried.

"We may get wet," Miriam said as she reached the buggy.

When she glanced at the sky, he saw a storm off to the north. It wouldn't hit the village, but it might come close to Harmony Creek.

Kyle again sat between him and Miriam as they headed home. Eli was grateful for his nephew's babbling about what he'd seen at the hardware store. That way Eli didn't have to make conversation with Miriam. How could he say anything when his wayward thoughts might burst out? She might consider him just another of her scholars. She was nice to him, but she was with everyone.

You should be glad, he told himself, but he wasn't.

After dropping Miriam off at her house and collecting the strawberries, Eli continued toward the far end of the hollow. They'd gotten home without any rain, and the storm was heading east into Vermont.

"Look!" cried Kyle, almost standing.

Eli put out an arm to keep the boy in his seat, but stared in astonishment at their home. The big oak had fallen between the house and the barn. The storm's winds must have toppled it. The top branches had clipped the roof of the house, ripping off shingles. Two windows on the second floor were shattered—one in his bedroom and the other in Kyle's. Debris was scattered everywhere, leaves, branches and pieces of wood that looked as if they would crumble if touched. Where the tree had broken, decayed wood was visible along the trunk.

In addition, the road to the barn was blocked. He couldn't drive his buggy inside or put Slim in his stall.

Turning the buggy wasn't easy at the narrow end of the road, but Slim seemed as eager to get away from the damage as Eli. Kyle, for once, was silent as they drove in the direction they'd come.

The tools Eli needed to fix the house were at the school. He hoped Miriam would watch Kyle while Caleb and more of his neighbors helped him clear away the broken tree.

Miriam threw open the front door as they got out of the buggy. "Eli! Why are you here? Did you forget something?"

Kyle pushed past him and threw his arms around her.

For the first time Eli was envious of his nephew as the boy embraced his teacher, talking nonstop about the damage at the end of the hollow.

"A tree?" she asked, looking over Kyle's head to Eli for confirmation.

Behind her, Caleb appeared, his face drawn with anxiety. "Has something happened, Eli?"

He answered them at the same time by explaining what he and Kyle had come home to find.

"I didn't guess the wind would be that strong at your end of the creek," Caleb said.

"The tree has a lot of rot on one side. I don't think it took too much wind to knock it over."

"If you had been at home and Kyle out playing…" Miriam shuddered and again he had to fight the yearning to draw her close so he could comfort her. "Thank the *gut* Lord it happened while we were in town."

"I'll head over to the Kuhnses' sawmill," Caleb said. "They've got a couple of chain saws." He paused. "What about the roof? Will you need a tarp?"

"*Ja*, and plywood to put over the broken windows. There are pieces left over at the school."

"Use whatever you need." He rushed out the door to alert their neighbors.

"Miriam, will you watch Kyle?" Eli asked.

"For as long as you need. *Komm* for supper." She gave him a weak smile. "We'll have strawberry shortcake, then you and Kyle can stay here tonight."

"You don't have room for guests."

"We'll make room."

He knew better than to argue when she stood with her hands at her waist and her chin had that determined line. And he was grateful his nephew wouldn't see the inside of the house and the full extent of the damage until after it was cleaned up.

His nephew grinned. "Will you read me a story and tuck me in at bedtime?"

She faltered as if the air had been drawn out of her, and her expression fell into what had to be regret or grief. Her arms wrapped around her middle in a protective pose. For a second. She straightened again. By sheer will, if Eli had to guess.

"We'll see," she said, and he wished he could better discern her tone. "Lots to do before then, ain't so?"

"But I can't wait to find out what happens to the boy and girl in the story you've been reading at school. Do they get down from the top of the mountain?"

She wagged a finger at his nephew, once again self-assured and playful. "Letting you hear before the others wouldn't be fair, would it?" With a laugh, she urged him to put the strawberries away so they stayed fresh.

As Kyle went to put the bowl in the refrigerator, Eli found himself lost in Miriam's eyes again. He stepped forward and cupped her cheek. He ran his thumb across her lower lip. It was as silken soft as he'd imagined while he'd stared at her mouth during their lessons... and other times, too.

The slamming of the refrigerator door brought him to his senses. He dropped his hand and hurried outside. Only when he reached the schoolhouse and was searching for pieces of plywood to cover the broken windows did he realize she hadn't halted his questing touch. He grinned. Maybe she felt something more for him than friendship. He intended to find out.

Chapter Ten

Miriam waited while her three friends edged past her and stepped out of Hank's van. She climbed out into the cloying heat and turned as the retired farmer called out to them.

"You said you wanted me to pick you up at the carnival grounds at nine." He rubbed his fingers against his chin. "Are you sure you don't want to stay and watch the fireworks?"

When Annie shot a glance at her, Miriam wanted to sigh. She understood more and more how much Caleb wished someone else would step forward to be the settlement's leader. Somehow, though she didn't know when or how or why, Miriam had been made the leader of the Spinsters' Club.

But Annie should understand why Hank was confused. Miriam had become so used to having Hank in their lives that she'd forgotten Hank, as an *Englischer*, used daylight saving time.

"You're right, Hank," she replied, not bothering to explain the simple mistake. "We're going to want to stay for the fireworks."

"They're scheduled for around nine thirty, but sometimes they don't get started until around ten. I'll be getting there a little before that to find a good place to watch. There's a dead-end street close to the carnival grounds. I should be able to find a parking space on it later in the evening. Look for the van after the fireworks. It should be easy to find. I'll let you know if I have to park somewhere else." He looked past them. "There's got to be ten times the number of vehicles in town today than usual."

And twenty times as many people as she'd ever seen before, Miriam realized as she and her friends crossed at the stoplight so they could stand in front of the library to watch the parade. Or that was where they'd planned to stand. It was obvious between the crowd gathered there and the raised table where two men and a woman were seated, it wouldn't be a *gut* place for her and her friends to view the parade.

The handwritten signs on the chairs announced the people at the table were judges. She wasn't sure what they were going to judge, but she heard spectators talking about floats in the parade.

Annie said, "It was nice of Hank to ask us about staying for the fireworks."

"Because he wants to watch them, too." Leanna winked at Miriam.

Her twin made a face. "Why didn't he say so?"

Miriam shrugged. "Who knows why men do any of the things they do?"

She regretted the words as soon as she spoke them, because the other three women stopped and regarded her with curiosity.

"Is something wrong? I thought you and Eli were

getting along well," said Leanna, ever the romantic. "He and his nephew have been over at your house most evenings, and you invited them to stay with you and Caleb until their house was safe to live in again."

"You know why they've come over in the evening. I'm teaching Eli to read lips."

Annie tapped her own. "Read my lips." She made a loud, smacking sound. "Kiss me, my darling."

Heat rose up Miriam's face and the twins began to giggle when an *Englisch* woman regarded them as if they'd lost their minds. They must be if they were discussing such things on the sidewalk where anyone could hear. Though they spoke in *Deitsch* among themselves, the teasing tones and the laughter spoke the truth in any language. And there were *Englisch* words interspersed, words they'd learned first in *Englisch* or had no real equivalent in *Deitsch*.

"They haven't been at the house the last couple of nights," Miriam said. "Eli's cleared away enough of the downed tree so they could get to the house. He's already made temporary repairs. Caleb said it was a real blessing nothing was badly damaged."

"Or no one." Sarah took Miriam's hand and squeezed it, the motion speaking more loudly than any words.

Aiming a smile at her friend, Miriam motioned with her head along the street. She kept taking surreptitious glances in every direction as she walked with her friends. Had Eli and Kyle arrived yet? They'd spent two nights with her and Caleb, and she hadn't had a chance to talk to Eli since then. Kyle gave her updates every day on the repairs his *onkel* had completed, and she guessed Eli would be back to work at the schoolhouse tomorrow to finish up the last few things before the scholars could use it.

Her skin tingled when she recalled how Eli's fingers had caressed her cheek before slipping along her lips. If Kyle closing the refrigerator door hadn't interrupted, would Eli have kissed her? Would she have let him?

She sighed as she thought of her reaction to his nephew's simple request for her to read to him and tuck him in. Eli had taken note of it. She was grateful he'd refrained from asking her why she'd acted as she had. Otherwise, she would have had to spill the past she wanted to put behind her for *gut*. But she couldn't forget the joy of putting Ralph to bed at her house when Yost had been too far away to get home before the boy's bedtime. It had happened more and more as their wedding day approached, but she'd seen it as a chance to spend extra time with Ralph. She'd also wanted to be supportive of Yost's business that had, for reasons he'd never explained, required him to be away several nights each week.

But cuddling the little boy and listening to his prayers and reading him to sleep had ended along with her betrothal.

Miriam shoved those memories away. Today wasn't for letting the past swallow her again. It was for enjoying a celebration with neighbors, both *Englisch* and plain.

Where were Eli and Kyle? She saw no sign of them.

Sweat bubbled on her forehead as they continued along the street. Maybe she should have worn her black bonnet, but the brim wouldn't have offered much of a reprieve from the sun in the cloudless sky. She breathed a sigh of relief when she stepped into the shade from the trees between the sidewalk and the road.

Finding a cool spot, she stood by her friends and waited for the parade to start…and for Eli to arrive.

Eli led his horse into one of the empty bays in the old firehouse. He saw two other buggies parked out front, one of them LaVon's bright yellow one. Miriam and her friends had arranged for the van to bring them into Salem. Had others done something similar? He hoped more people from the new settlement would come to enjoy the evening. Kyle had told him for the past few days the *kinder* had discussed nothing other than the parade and upcoming carnival. As the events began after milking should be done, a tradition from a time when *Englischers* worked the small farms that surrounded the village, the other families along Harmony Creek should be arriving soon.

Looking at his nephew, who was rocking from one foot to the other in his excitement, he grinned. Kyle must have checked the clock in the kitchen every five minutes, waiting for when they would leave for the village.

Eli motioned for his nephew to follow him toward the street. The parade's start time was still almost a half hour away, and Kyle wasn't the only one excited about it. Other *kinder* raced along the sidewalks edging the road and the parking lanes that were wide enough for two cars.

Or one big tractor and a flatbed trailer, he realized when he looked north along Main Street and saw the equipment parked in front of the small, red building. It had been built as a movie theater decades before and now served as a *doktor*'s office. A small structure that appeared to be made out of cardboard and construction paper sat in the middle of the flatbed where hay bales had probably been stacked a few days ago.

Two popcorn wagons, their silver sides glinting in the sunshine and the aroma of butter and salt the best advertisement of their wares, were parked on opposite sides of the street. Lines snaked away from them as people waited to buy popcorn, peanuts and other treats.

Eli sensed the curious glances aimed at him and his nephew. Unlike the *Englischers*, who were dressed in shorts and casual T-shirts and baseball caps, they wore dark brown broadfall trousers, light blue shirts and their straw hats. He nodded to people he recognized from doing errands in the village and smiled at others.

"Have you ever seen so many people?" Kyle asked as he held tightly to Eli's hand so they didn't get separated in the crowd clogging the sidewalk. "Everyone in the county must be here. Maybe the whole state."

"And beyond." He was amazed at how easily he discerned what his nephew was saying. Miriam had been correct. Before he had begun lessons with her, he'd already been reading lips without being aware of it.

Kyle bounced on every step as they headed south toward where there were some open places among the crowd where they could get a *gut* view of the parade. The stoplight at the intersection of Main and Broadway was being ignored while two county sheriffs directed cars and pedestrians. Other officers would halt traffic going through the village while the bands and floats followed the parade route toward the carnival grounds on Archibald Street.

They found a spot close to the bridge over White

Creek. As Eli glanced at the shallow water flowing between two stone walls, he thought of the stories he'd been told about how a hurricane a few years before had turned that trickle into a torrent. Water had spread out more than a quarter of a mile across the village, turning Broadway, the street that became the road running past Harmony Hollow, into a raging river. Dozens of homes had been damaged.

Tonight the creek flowed innocently beneath the bridge. A few fish darted through the clear water. When Kyle noticed them, he leaned against the concrete wall and stood on his tiptoes.

Eli resisted the urge to warn him to be careful. He couldn't be overprotective, but kept glancing toward his nephew until someone tapped Eli's arm.

His heart jumped. Hoping Miriam was trying to get his attention, he turned to see a tall, thin *Englischer* with a graying mustache and a navy baseball cap with a bright B in the center.

Boston Red Sox, Eli translated. The baseball team in Boston was another subject that transfixed Kyle.

"Are you the Amish carpenter?" asked the man. "Eli Troyer?"

He nodded. "That's me."

"Tuck Rossi over at the hardware store said you were looking for work. Do you have a business card?" The man didn't give him a chance to answer before going on. "My wife has been reminding me that we need to do something about our sagging sunporch. Is that something you could take care of?"

"I can tell you once I've had a chance to examine the porch."

"Can you stop by soon?" The *Englischer* grinned. "I'm John Osborne, by the way."

"How about the day after tomorrow in the morning?" It was the best time for Eli because Kyle would be at school.

John agreed so eagerly Eli guessed the porch must be in dire condition. Getting the man's address, which was close to where the carnival was being held on Archibald Street, Eli shook John's proffered hand before John went across the street to where an elderly woman and a bunch of *kinder* stood. When the youngsters greeted John with enthusiasm, Eli guessed they were John's *kins-kinder*.

"Who was that?" asked Kyle as he pushed away from the bridge to move to where he could see the parade.

"A man who may have a job for me."

The boy's eyes widened. "And you were able to talk to him without me?"

"*Ja.* I've learned a lot from Miriam."

Kyle stared at the ground and mumbled something. When Eli was about to ask him to repeat it, a siren blared so loudly he couldn't miss it. He put his hands on his nephew's shoulders, ready to pull him back if a police car raced along the empty road.

It inched along the street instead. It must be the signal that the parade was about to begin. People around him clapped and cheered and called joking remarks to the two officers, who waved through the open windows.

Moments later the car was followed by a group of teenagers dressed in black trousers and white shirts with purple and gold scarves around their shoulders. They were playing a variety of musical instruments. He guessed they were the band from the local high school. He didn't recognize the song, but the band played it with enthusiasm as they marched with heads high. Several of the younger students were out of step, but the spectators cheered as they went past.

"You know what, *Onkel* Eli?" asked Kyle after tugging on his sleeve to get his attention.

"What?"

"We need to get some drums." He made motions with his hands as if he held drumsticks. "I could play them while you play your harmonica. It would sound great!"

"Definitely loud." He hadn't unpacked his harmonica since their arrival in the new settlement. Was this Kyle's way of saying it was long past due? Ruffling Kyle's hair, he said, "Look! Here comes the Salem Volunteer Fire Department."

The boy was enchanted by the antique horse-drawn pumper being pulled by two men in old-fashioned turnout gear and bright red T-shirts. The firefighters had buckets attached to their trousers, and they tossed candy to kids on both sides of the street. Kyle joined the others running to collect pieces of hard candy and gum.

Eli smiled when his nephew offered a toddler boy a share of what he'd gotten.

The little boy grinned and selected a few pieces.

"What do you say?" his *mamm* prompted.

He assumed the *kind* said *danki*, because the woman smiled.

"Stick with me." Kyle puffed his thin chest out as he ruffled the *kind*'s hair as Eli had his. "We'll get more the next time." He pointed to his mouth where one of his upper teeth had fallen out that morning. "I'll give the sticky ones to you cuz my other tooth is loose."

Caught between being delighted at how much of the conversation he could understand as he looked from one person to another and his nephew remembering his lessons about sharing and helping others, Eli accepted the thanks the *Englisch* lady gave him.

"How cute is that?" asked Miriam as she stepped forward.

How long had she been standing nearby? Not long, he guessed, because Kyle waved in excitement when he saw her. As he had before, he rushed over to embrace her. The boy showed off the candy he'd picked up and motioned for her to help herself.

Eli didn't catch what Miriam and his nephew said to each other because their heads were bent together. He guessed she'd urged Kyle to enjoy his bounty. It wasn't easy to think about anything else when he had a *wunderbaar* excuse to look at her pretty features. Not just her lips, but her twinkling eyes and the gentle curve of her high cheekbones. Even with the heat, she managed to look fresh.

When Kyle saw a tractor and flatbed wagon approaching, he hurried to where the little boy was waiting for him. They grinned as candy flew off the float. Some things about the size of Kyle's fist were tossed, as well.

Kyle picked up one.

"You can have it," Kyle said as he handed the small red plastic tractor to the littler boy.

The *kind* beamed and jumped up and down with his excitement. He gave Kyle a big hug before spinning to show the toy to his *mamm*.

"That was very kind of you, Kyle," Miriam said.

"He's an *Englischer*, and it was an *Englisch* tractor," the boy replied with a youngster's logic.

The little boy tugged on Kyle's arm. When Kyle

looked at him, the *kind* smiled and said something Eli couldn't hear.

Miriam tapped Eli's arm. When he looked at her, she smiled. "Kyle's little friend said T-A-N-K E-W."

Eli chuckled along with her as the little boy went to stand beside his *mamm*. "They create a language all their own when they're little."

Kyle pointed at another trio of fire trucks rolling in the middle of the street. They were from three different nearby villages. He'd heard of Cambridge and Greenwich, but not Argyle. Each vehicle was met with shouts and cheers. When they blew their sirens or honked their resonant horns, he wasn't surprised Kyle and the little boy and half of the other spectators put their hands over their ears. The sound blared through his hearing aids, but he didn't turn them down. He didn't want to miss a moment of the excitement.

"Kyle told me that you're about finished repairing the house," Miriam said as the trucks rolled past.

"The roof didn't take long to repair, and the tree's been cleared away. Plenty of *gut* firewood for next winter."

She gave an emoted shudder. "I want to enjoy summer before I think about cold weather again."

"Agreed." He couldn't halt the thought of holding her close on a cold winter night. Sitting by the stove in his house on the simple sofa he'd rescued from the used furniture dealer, he'd put his arm around her shoulders and invite her to lean her head against him. They wouldn't have to talk. Just being together would make him happy.

As it did now.

He was saved from his own fantasy by the arrival of the next float. It was filled with *kinder* and decorated to look like a dairy barn. Two teenage girls wore lacy gowns, and two younger ones were dressed in black-and-white and had horns on their heads. The latter he guessed were supposed to be cows that belonged to the other boys and girls who wore overalls and straw hats.

Farmers, he was sure.

That was confirmed when he saw the sign on the side of the decorated hay wagon. The two in the fancy gowns were that year's Washington County Dairy Princess and the runner-up to the title. The girls waved, and the younger *kinder* threw more candy toward the spectators.

Again, Kyle took the little boy by the hand and helped him gather up pieces. They giggled together and compared what they'd gotten.

A bigger boy reached around the little boy and snatched the candy out of his hand. The *kind* began to cry.

Kyle stepped toward the boy, then paused. He glanced over his shoulder at his *onkel*.

Eli said nothing. Kyle knew the importance of not getting into fights. He'd been taught he must turn the other cheek and avoid any violence, no matter the circumstances. Still, his nephew needed to make such a decision himself.

The taller boy stuck out his chin as if daring Kyle to hit him. The nearby adults looked on in shock.

By Kyle's sides, his hands started to curl into fists. He halted himself and turned to the little boy. Holding out his right hand with several types of candy to the *kind*, he yelped when the bigger boy grabbed Kyle's candy, too, and then laughed.

That laughter disappeared when a man in a deputy sheriff's uniform stepped forward and grabbed the boy by the shoulder. The deputy was such a broad man, the boy who'd taken the candy seemed puny in comparison.

"Did I see you steal candy from these boys?" the deputy asked. Without giving him a chance to answer, he growled, "Give it back and apologize."

"Sorry," mumbled the boy as he handed Kyle the candy.

Kyle gave it to the little boy as the deputy ordered, "Say it louder."

"Sorry," repeated the boy, kicking at a loose stone. It skittered onto the road.

Kyle stepped forward and looked at the tall deputy. "Sir, he can have my candy if he wants it."

The deputy was speechless, and other people around them looked even more astonished.

"I've got plenty," Kyle continued, and Eli realized his nephew had mistaken the man's amazement for hesitation to accept the offer from a *kind* he didn't know. "If he wants it, he can have it."

"But he was going to steal it from you and that little guy," said the deputy.

"I know, but it's important we forgive those who trespass against us." He looked at the boy who was half a head taller than he was. "If you want my candy, you can have it." He held up his left hand and unfolded his fingers to reveal five pieces.

The boy took one, then a second piece. "Thanks."

"Your boy?" asked the deputy, looking at Eli.

"Ja." It wasn't easy to keep his pride with Kyle out of his voice. He hoped God would forgive him for the burst of *hochmut.*

"You've taught him well."

Eli nodded his thanks, and the deputy walked away, herding the boy ahead of him.

When another float came by and balloons floated out to be batted among the spectators, Miriam gave him a smile that seemed to reach inside him and soothe the pain that had been his companion for the past four years. He didn't notice when a balloon bounced off his head or Kyle's laughter as he hit it to someone else. All he saw was her smile.

"The policeman is right," she said. "You have taught Kyle well."

"I've tried."

"And succeeded. I've worked with *kinder* since I was sixteen, and not many of them—whether plain or *Englisch*—would be so forgiving and generous. Kyle is blessed to have you in his life." She took his hand and held it between both of hers. "And so am I."

When she released his hand and began to laugh as she looked at where Kyle was again helping the littler boy gather a collection of candy and small toys, Eli wished he had an excuse to touch her again. He was determined to find a way before the night was over.

Chapter Eleven

Miriam was glad she and Eli held Kyle's hands as they walked in the middle of the street. No vehicle traffic was allowed on the route the parade had followed. With the rush of people, she wondered how anyone could have gone in the opposite direction.

Though only one side of the street had a sidewalk, people walked on both, tramping through front yards, as well as down the road. Every front porch was filled with celebrants who'd had great seats for the parade that passed right by their homes. American flags flew from almost every house, and some were decked with bunting. Decorative banners hung at the front of about half of the houses with appliquéd pictures of balloons and puppies and summer scenes.

Behind the houses, Miriam saw the flat wagons used for floats parked out of the way. Tissue paper and streamers fluttered in the evening breeze, and pieces that had escaped from chicken wire and staples bounced along the ground.

"Be careful there," called a woman.

Miriam looked at the porch to her right. Two *kinder*

were trying to edge past a trio of tables where cakes, pies and plates of cookies were arranged. How many guests was the family expecting?

She got her answer when another woman stopped at the bottom of the steps and held up a cake topped by coconut frosting. The woman with the cake apologized for being so late with her contribution to the cake auction.

Scanning the tables, Miriam smiled when she saw the donations from her friends in the Spinsters' Club. Annie had made a cake that looked as stunning as something Caleb might have made. Sarah's wasn't as fancy, but the bright green frosting made it stand out. Leanna had sent a heaping plate of chocolate chip cookies.

Caleb had delivered all the goodies earlier in the afternoon before crowds made it impossible to navigate with a cake in each hand. She walked toward the porch to admire the variety and quantity of cakes. There must be almost two dozen arranged on the table.

"Which one is yours?" asked Eli when he came to stand beside her.

"That one," Kyle said before she could answer. He pointed to a round cake with grape jelly as well as buttercream frosting. "I'm right, ain't so?"

She was astonished, and as she nodded, she could tell Eli was, too.

"Don't be surprised," the boy said. "That's the same grape jelly you sent to us the day we arrived."

"Kyle," Miriam said, putting a hand on his arm when she saw Eli struggling to understand what the *kind* had said. "Slow and simple, remember?"

His nephew nodded and spoke slower. "It is the purplest purple I've ever seen." He looked at her. When she smiled, he looked as proud as if he'd been the grand marshal of the parade.

"In all your six years?" asked Eli.

"*Ja.* I have eaten lots and lots of jelly sandwiches." His grin widened. "Lots and lots and lots."

"Which is why you're growing like a weed." Eli tapped the top of his nephew's straw hat. "This is going to be even with mine soon."

The boy grinned.

"Aren't you a firefighter?" the woman on the porch asked Eli.

"*Ja.* Yes, ma'am, I am."

"Good. You're here just in time. We need to get the rest of these donations to the carnival for the sweets auction."

Miriam grinned as Eli looked at her and arched his brows. He didn't say anything to her as he climbed the two steps and asked, "How can I help?"

"Wait right there." The woman called to two younger *Englisch* women who'd been chatting on the other side of the porch.

As they walked to the table, they admired Eli, though they looked away if his eyes shifted in their direction.

Miriam despised the twinge of something unpleasant in her middle. She didn't like how the women were boldly ogling Eli and how he politely smiled in return. She was glad when the older woman returned with two cut-down cardboard boxes.

After putting two cakes in each box, she set the wider one on top of the other. She held them out to Eli.

"Here you go," the woman said. "Thank you for helping, young man."

Kyle laughed at his *onkel* being addressed as a young

man, but couldn't hide how much he wished he was old enough to tote a box himself to the carnival.

They continued along the street with Kyle walking a couple of steps ahead to clear a path for Eli and the cakes. When Miriam glanced back, she saw several other firefighters waiting to help with delivering the desserts to the carnival grounds. She smiled as the two young women flirted with them as they had with Eli.

She shouldn't have gotten upset over the flirts. Eli hadn't invited it, and the young women obviously were just having fun.

Grant me the wisdom to see the truth, Lord, not what I fear is happening. I will try to hand my fears to You, so I can come to see how infinitesimal they truly are.

"Are you all right?" asked Eli as he looked at her.

She hadn't realized she'd stopped while sending up her heartfelt prayer. "I'm doing fine. Let's go. I can't wait to see what you firefighters have devised for our entertainment tonight."

"I know what you mean." He winked at her and continued along the street. "I can't wait, either."

She matched his steps while anticipation bubbled through her as she looked forward to the evening to come. It was going to be *wunderbaar*.

The carnival grounds consisted of a half dozen white buildings. One was almost as large as the first floor of Miriam's house, but the others were narrow and only wide enough to hold two or three people. Open squares built of narrow boards were set in the center between the smaller buildings. Cars were parked in surprisingly even rows on the grass along with three buggies. Smells of hot dogs and hamburgers and sweets reached out to lure them into the carnival.

Eli was astonished how many people had come to the carnival grounds. The few permanent buildings housed games for *kinder* and adults who were young at heart. A long line was in front of the open area where players could test their skill at sinking a miniature basketball in a small hoop. When someone managed to make a basket, shouts resounded over the music from a deejay.

Once he'd delivered the boxes to the biggest building where the cake auction would be held in a few hours, he set off to explore the carnival with Miriam and Kyle. He wasn't sure which of them was the most excited to be there. As they walked around, trying not be separated by the eddies of people, they looked in the booths.

"They're all skill games," Miriam said with a big grin. "Putting a ring around a bottle top or tossing a coin on a dish or breaking a balloon with a dart. I didn't expect that." Laughing, she added, "I didn't know what would be here, so everything is a surprise."

"So you're not going to try to win a goldfish by tossing a Ping-Pong ball in a bowl?"

She laughed again. "Caleb has been talking about getting a dog, and I can see the dog lapping water out of the poor fish's bowl."

Kyle grabbed his arm. "Look, *Onkel* Eli. That man is saying anyone can win a stuffed toy by knocking over three burlap cats. Can I try?"

"It won't be as easy as they make it sound," he warned.

"But I throw *gut*." He puffed out his thin chest. "I've pitched twice at school."

Putting his arm around his nephew's shoulders, he

said, "You can try it once. There are other games I know you'll want to play, too."

Kyle rushed to the firefighter who was manning the booth and gave him two quarters. As the firefighter, one Eli hadn't met yet, handed three baseballs to the boy, he asked, "Who's going to throw?"

"Me!" Kyle grinned and bounced from one foot to the other. He dropped one of the balls, but Miriam snagged it before it could roll far away.

While Kyle took his place to throw, Eli introduced himself to the other man. They watched, along with Miriam, as Kyle drew back his arm to throw the ball at the stuffed burlap cats set in a pyramid on a narrow shelf.

The boy grunted as he hurled. The ball bounced off one cat, which rocked but didn't tumble off the shelf. The next two balls sailed over the uppermost cat.

Kyle didn't say anything as he shuffled aside to let the next thrower have his turn.

Eli debated between consoling his nephew and saying nothing. He wasn't sure which he should do.

Beside him, Miriam didn't seem to have any qualms. "That first throw was *gut*, Kyle."

"It didn't knock the cats over."

"No, but you did hit one. If you'd been throwing in a ball game, that would have been a strike."

"It would have been, wouldn't it?" The *kind* perked up. "Who wants a stuffed dog anyhow? I'd rather be a *gut* pitcher."

Eli smiled at Miriam over the little boy's head. She was *wunderbaar* with *kinder*, and she would be a great *mamm* someday.

No, he wasn't going to think of the future. He wanted to enjoy the evening.

Had he missed his chance, he wondered when Miriam excused herself and went to talk to her friends? He couldn't monopolize her time, though the bare light bulbs hanging from wires strung from booth to booth and across the center didn't seem so bright and festive when she walked away.

Taking Kyle by the hand, he went with his nephew to the next booth. It was identical to the previous one, except there were three pyramids of empty vegetable cans. Two air guns rested on the board across the front of the booth at the perfect height for a teen to rest an elbow on while firing. A wooden crate waited for young *kinder* to use.

"Try this, Kyle." Eli paid Chief Pulaski, who was in charge of the booth, then handed an air gun to the boy. "Aim at a can. One at a time."

Kyle climbed on the crate before taking the air gun with the piece of cork stuck into the barrel. He hefted it to his shoulder and leaned his elbow on the edge of the booth.

Eli held his breath as the boy did before squeezing the trigger. The small chunk of cork hit the empty can, knocking it off the others. He did the same with his second shot, but the third one missed.

"Good shooting, young man," Chief Pulaski said. "You need to have your uncle bring you to the gun safety course at the courthouse as soon as you're eight years old. You'll learn to handle guns and have a chance to shoot them."

"Can I?" Kyle asked, his eyes glittering like the stars appearing in the sky.

"Ask me again when you are eight," Eli said, taking the gun and handing it to the chief. "Until then, no guns for you. Except if you want to visit this booth again next year."

Kyle's grin was almost too wide for his young face when he took the plastic whistle the chief held out to him.

"Go ahead," the older man said. "Try it out and make sure it works."

The boy put the whistle to his lips and blew. Its shrill squeal silenced the people around them.

"Are you trying to convince the firefighters to get rid of their sirens and give you the job?" asked Eli.

"He's loud enough," the chief replied. "Better put it in your pocket, son, and save it for when you get home." He winked at Eli. "That way, you'll disturb only a few people at a time."

Eli laughed, though the shrill sound had been intensified painfully by his hearing aids. Taking Kyle's hand again, he continued around the carnival, which seemed to be growing more crowded by the minute.

When they passed a roped-off area where a girl was walking a horse around in a circle with a small *kind* on its back, Kyle said, "Next year let's bring a horse and give rides."

"We don't have a saddle horse."

"Yet. We're going to get one, ain't so?"

"Ja." He smiled at his nephew, knowing how much the boy missed riding their neighbor's pony in Delaware. "Once we build another stall in the barn, we'll start looking around for a pony."

Kyle shook his head. "A horse. I'm getting too big for a pony."

"Let's see what we can find." He turned to see Miriam and her friends strolling toward them.

His nephew raced toward her, edging around people and managing not to bump into anyone. When Kyle showed her the whistle he'd won at the shooting booth, Eli didn't have to see his face to know he was telling her everything about the experience.

Sarah, Annie and Leanna greeted Eli with smiles when he joined their group. Though he saw the curiosity in their eyes as they looked from him to Miriam, none of them asked any questions.

When Annie invited him to join them for the cake auction, he agreed...a few seconds after Kyle gave his enthusiastic answer. His nephew grinned at him, and Eli wondered if the boy had picked out the cake he wanted his *onkel* to bid on. If it was the one Miriam had made, that was sure to cause talk, but the funds were going to the fire department and he could put up with *gut*-natured teasing.

The women found a spot off to the left of the building where they would have an excellent view of the auctioneer, who was the assistant fire chief Robert Quartermaine. The firemen called him "Q" not because of his name, but because, as they'd told Eli, the assistant chief was as bald as a cue ball.

Miriam motioned to him and Kyle. "Don't bid on my cake. I'll make you one if you'd like. Buy someone else's cake, so you can sample something different."

Eli nodded, wondering if she'd made the offer to keep from putting them in an embarrassing situation. He told himself to stop looking for ulterior motives. She was being nice, and he should appreciate that and enjoy her company.

Now *that* was a plan for the evening.

* * *

Miriam gazed at the overhead lights and the moths dancing around them. Everyone and everything was having fun at the carnival. Walking through the crowd that hadn't diminished though it was getting late, she took care her cotton candy didn't get bumped. The sticky froth would cement itself to clothing or hair.

She smiled when Eli and Kyle walked toward her. The two were deep in conversation. Kyle continued, she noticed, to make the same type of motions he had before Eli began reading lips. A habit? She wondered if the boy realized what he was doing. When she had the opportunity, she'd speak to Eli about it. Not in front of his nephew, because she didn't want to embarrass the *kind*.

They paused to look at the ground, and Miriam watched how Eli pointed out something to the boy. Anyone seeing them together couldn't fail to notice the strong bond between the tall, broad-shouldered man and the little boy. In the stark light from the bare bulbs overhead, glints in Eli's hair were almost as bright red as Kyle's ginger hair.

Eli stood straighter, and his gaze found hers over the people walking between them. He walked toward her, his eyes glowing with the special warmth that urged her to believe in love again. Knowing she was risking her heart, his smile and easy gait dared her to throw caution aside.

When he stopped in front of her, he asked, "Have you been having a *gut* time with your friends?"

"Ja." It was the truth. There was no reason to tell him that, even while she was walking around with the other members of the Spinsters' Club, she'd watched for any glimpse of him and his nephew.

Kyle skipped to them. "What's that?"

"This?" She smiled. "It's cotton candy and my weakness. I can't resist it." She offered the column of spun sugar to Kyle and then to Eli.

They each took a small piece. When his nephew's eyes widened as they savored the sweetness, Eli reached into his pocket.

"How much is it?" he asked.

"A dollar," she replied.

He handed four quarters to Kyle. "Meet us here as soon as you get your cotton candy."

"Danki," the boy shouted over his shoulder as he ran toward where the spun sugar was being sold.

"He said—"

He interrupted Miriam. "I guessed what he said."

"You're getting much better at reading lips and body language."

"I'm trying."

She offered him another bite of the cotton candy. When he looked at his fingers that were already stained blue, he shook his head with a grin. He did sample a small piece of Kyle's pink cotton candy when the boy came back to them.

A man followed him. She realized it was Lyndon Wagler, who was a couple years older than his twin sisters, Annie and Leanna. With him was his son, also named Lyndon but called Junior. He and Kyle sat next to each other during school.

Miriam picked at her cotton candy as Lyndon talked to Eli, and Kyle showed off his whistle to his friend. She could wander away and find her friends, but she didn't because she wanted to spend more time with Eli.

"We're going fishing in the morning," Lyndon said.

"Junior is wondering if Kyle would like to spend the night tonight and go with us."

Junior added, "*Komm* over, Kyle. We'll have a lot of fun, and *Daed* says we can cook the fish we catch."

When Kyle hesitated, Miriam was bewildered. She'd expected Kyle to leap at the chance to join his friend.

"That sounds like fun," Eli said. "Go if you'd like, Kyle."

"I can stay and help you understand what's going on," Kyle said.

"I'm fine. Go and have fun. If I need help talking to someone, Miriam will help me."

The boy hesitated, an odd look on his face, and then nodded before he walked away with Lyndon and Junior.

Watching them, Miriam said, "Kyle has had too much responsibility for too long." She put her fingers to her lips, but lowered them as she added, "I didn't mean to criticize."

"You aren't saying anything I haven't thought," Eli replied. "That's why I wanted him to go and have fun."

"You're a *gut onkel.*"

"And you've got blue lips." He laughed. "Someone would think you were freezing to death."

Teasing each other, they walked to where people were gathering to watch the fireworks that would be shot off in the next half hour. Eli knew an excellent place to view them and asked her to go with him. She agreed, stopping long enough to let her friends know she would meet them at the van later. She hoped Eli didn't notice the knowing grins the other young women exchanged.

Eli led her past Hank's van. The driver was standing beside it, bending another man's ear. Not slowing,

Eli walked to the end of the street and the cornfield beyond it. The young stalks of corn stood higher than her knees, a *gut* sign according to farmers' old adage of having corn be "knee-high by the Fourth of July" in order to get an abundant harvest before the first frost.

A fire engine was parked at the edge of the field. He called a greeting to his fellow firefighters. They were leaning against the engine in nonchalant poses, but they'd leap into action if a firework fell to the ground and ignited the grass.

She enjoyed talking with Eli as they waited for the show to begin. The street behind them became thick with spectators, and she was glad he'd suggested finding a spot when he did. Anticipation became almost tangible as the clock ticked past the scheduled starting time, but nobody complained.

Then with a *whoosh* and a *boom* that rattled the windows of the houses along the street, the first rocket exploded into shades of red, white and blue.

"Wow!" Miriam gasped.

Eli turned down his hearing aids as he said, "You're supposed to say 'Oooo' first, then 'Aaaah.'"

She looked at him, then at the sky as another explosion, this one bright white, scattered the darkness. "I didn't know there were rules."

"I didn't, either, but Kyle informed me today that was how I was supposed to react when the fireworks were set off." He paused as another thud followed an explosion that looked like a giant, golden weeping willow in the sky.

Too soon the show was over. Everyone clapped and shouted before turning to return to their cars and homes. The Fourth of July celebrations were over for another year.

When Eli didn't follow the others, Miriam asked, "Do you need to help with cleanup at the carnival grounds?"

"That's scheduled for tomorrow. The new guys are expected to put in a few hours." His voice softened as he said, "I know you're planning on going home with your friends. But I'm headed that way, too, and if you'd like, you can ride with me. The evening's been too much fun to let it end now."

Her heart did a pirouette in her chest. "*Ja, danki.* I'd like that."

He smiled, and she was sure every bone inside her melted. Oh, she was getting in way too deep! *It's just a ride home with a friend.* She was trying to delude herself. And failing big-time. She was thrilled to imagine sitting beside him in his buggy as they drove through the humid night.

"Slim is at the old firehouse next to the library. It's far enough away so the fireworks shouldn't have spooked him." He readjusted his hearing aids and held out his hand. "Shall we go and see how he's doing?"

She started to put hers in it, then paused. "Before we go, I need to let my friends know so they do not wait and wait for me by the van."

"Your Harmony Creek Spinsters' Club friends?"

Fire erupted up Miriam's face as Eli grinned. In the streetlight's glow, she could see his eyes twinkling. She resisted her urge to cross her arms in front of her and meet his gaze. He'd become too skilled at reading body language, and she didn't want to give him any clue to her embarrassment.

"How do you know that name?" she asked in a careful tone.

"Menno heard his sister talking with the Wagler twins, and one of them mentioned the four of you had started a frolic group called the Harmony Creek Spinsters' Club."

"The name is a joke."

"I guessed that, but it's a joke I like because I have never seen your cheeks so rosy before."

"You can't see that at night."

"I can imagine it." He ran a crooked finger along her left cheek. "And I can feel it."

Aware of how many people lingered along the street, she lowered her head, though his touch was beyond delightful. She went to the van, but only Hank was there. She asked him to tell her friends she had another ride home. He nodded and returned to his conversation. She was relieved she didn't have to see her friends' smiles that warned her they were planning to tease her the next time they were together. At least Eli wouldn't witness it.

Together they strolled back the way they'd come. When Eli took her hand, Miriam moved a half step closer to him. A few other people walked toward Main Street, and none of them paid any attention to her and Eli.

Moonlight streamed along the street as they headed north hand in hand. Cars went by, but the sidewalks were growing deserted beneath the bright moon and scattered stars. They stopped to collect Slim, who nickered a greeting at Eli's arrival. He hitched the horse and climbed into the buggy to sit beside her. Was he as aware as she was of how nothing was between them, not even his nephew?

By the time they reached the edge of the village, the only sounds beyond the peepers were the rattle of the wheels and the clatter of Slim's horseshoes on the asphalt. Eli reached out and took her hand, drawing her along the seat to him. Leaning her head on his shoulder, she gazed at the stars poking through the darkness above the mountains.

The buggy slowed to make the turn onto the road along the creek. When he drew in the horse, stopping them, she asked if everything was all right.

Instead of replying, he contracted his arm to tilt her toward him. His fingers beneath her chin brought her face toward his. He gave her no time to protest, though she couldn't have imagined uttering a single word as she looked into his moonlit face. He slanted his mouth across hers. The enthralling sensation of his lips on hers banished every thought but of the moment. As his lips thrilled hers, her fingers slid to curve around his shoulders. She clasped her hands at his nape, and he showered kisses across her cheeks until she laughed with joy.

He drew back enough to say, "You taste as sweet as cotton candy."

"Because I had some, remember?"

"No, that's not what I meant. Maybe I should have said cotton candy tastes as sweet as you."

He claimed her lips again, and she welcomed his kiss, for once not caring what she was risking.

Chapter Twelve

Eli woke smiling. The memory of the buggy ride home last night was as *wunderbaar* as his favorite dream, but it'd been real. For so long he'd imagined holding Miriam to his heart. When it had happened, she'd been more splendid in his embrace than he'd been able to guess. He'd given her another kiss when he dropped her off at her house. It had whetted his yearning for more kisses.

He wondered when he could ask her to go for a ride with him again. Would tonight be too soon?

Sitting, he stretched to switch on the propane light atop his bedside table. He yawned as he got up and dressed. Staying out late with a pretty girl and then rising early in the morning to do chores was something that had seemed easy when he was a young man.

But he wasn't old. He'd turned thirty-one a few months ago. Yet, in some ways, it felt as if he'd lived a complete lifetime in the past four years since his brother's death. He couldn't remember the last time he hadn't felt the weight of his obligations pressing on him. He needed to be a *gut* member of the new settlement's *Leit*, to rear Kyle and to do his best for anyone who hired him. He'd been able to forget all that while he held Miriam in his arms.

By the time Eli finished getting ready for the new day, he realized he was whistling. He couldn't remember the last time he'd done that. He didn't stop as he started *kaffi*. He broke two eggs into a cast-iron pan and began scrambling them. Making bacon, he put it on a plate while he fried toast. He spooned the scrambled eggs over the toast and carried the plate to the table. Pouring a cup of *kaffi*, he took milk out of the refrigerator and put both beside his plate that looked so alone on the big table.

He realized it was the first time he'd eaten breakfast without Kyle almost since the boy was born. As he bent his head to say silent grace, he added a prayer of thanks that God had brought Kyle a *gut* friend. He looked toward an eastern window. The sun was rising, and the boys should be having fun fishing on such a pleasant morning.

Eli drove with Menno to the carnival grounds to help his fellow firefighters empty the metal barrels that had served as trash cans. He found coins that had either fallen out of someone's pocket or skittered off one of the low platforms where quarters had been tossed at glasses and bowls. By the time he finished just before midday, he'd collected almost ten dollars, which he gave to Chief Pulaski to add to the firehouse's coffers. Others picked up change, too, increasing the profits for the carnival.

He left Menno at the Waglers' farm and went to his own. As he did each time he drove in, he glanced at the stack of firewood from the tree that had crashed into the house. He was grateful the repairs had been quick and that all the materials he needed had been available at Rossi's hardware store.

His stomach growled as he put Slim out to pasture. Going into the house, he considered what to have for his noon meal. He decided on a peanut butter and jelly sandwich with the last jar of Miriam's grape jelly.

He was about to take his first bite when the door opened. He grinned as Kyle walked in. "Did you catch a lot?"

"No." He grimaced. "Nothing was biting except mosquitoes."

"The cortisone is in the medicine cabinet upstairs. It'll take away the itch."

"I know."

Though Eli couldn't hear the boy's tone, it was easy to tell something more than a fruitless fishing trip was bothering Kyle. He looked as downtrodden as he had last night at the carnival grounds before he left with his friend. Was whatever had upset him last night still nettling him today? The boy's shoulders slumped, and he didn't meet Eli's eyes. More than once, he shifted as if he didn't want Eli to make out what he appeared to be muttering.

Eli gave him a chance to voice his distress while he made a second peanut butter and jelly sandwich. He put it and a handful of chips on a plate and set it in front of the boy. His nephew took a couple of bites and broke the potato chips into tiny pieces on his plate and moved them around with his fingertip.

Abruptly, Kyle pushed back from the table and ran into the living room.

About to call after him with a reminder Kyle needed to bow his head and share with God his gratitude for the meal before he left the table, Eli halted when he saw the little boy throw himself into the rocking chair so hard it almost tipped over.

Kyle gripped one of the vertical slats on the back and leaned his head against the rest. He didn't say anything. He didn't move. He stared at the wall.

Something had happened.

Something bad.

Eli stood, then paused to aim a prayer at God. It was an apology for being as remiss as his nephew at not showing his gratitude. However, most of his wordless prayer was asking God to give him the right words to help Kyle. The last time he'd seen his nephew sitting in the rocker like that was during the weeks after Milan and Shirley were killed. Then Kyle had spent hours in the chair, rocking and saying little.

He took one step toward the living room before the kitchen door opened.

Miriam carried in the cake she'd promised last night to make for them. She greeted him, but her smile faded when he didn't return it. Looking past him, he knew the exact moment when she saw Kyle curled into a ball, clinging to the chair. Dismay dimmed her eyes and stiffened her shoulders.

She set the cake on the table and untied her bonnet. Looking at him, she arched her brows in a silent query.

He raised his hands, palms up, in a shrug before walking to the rocker. Putting his hand on the top of the chair, he asked, "Won't you tell me what's wrong, Kyle?"

For a long minute Kyle said nothing. He bounced to his feet, his fingers curled into fists by his sides as they had during the parade. Not angry fists, but frustrated ones Eli realized when his nephew wailed, "Why did everything have to change?"

"I thought you liked living here in Harmony Creek."

"I do, but—" He hung his head.

Miriam said, "Your *onkel* can't hear you if you don't look at him."

Again Kyle hesitated, then his head jerked and his shoulders went back. He stood as stiffly as if he'd been turned into a statue. Tears filled his eyes and hung on his lashes.

"Living here isn't the only thing that's changed! We've changed. We used to be a team. You and me. That's what you've told me. Over and over. You said that you and I would always be a team."

"And we are. We always will be." He swallowed hard. His nephew's words pummeled him like a blow to the gut.

"No." His voice broke. "Not like we used to be. You don't need me anymore."

"What?" He should say more, but words deserted him.

"You know what everyone says. I'm glad you do, but you don't need me anymore. You've left me behind." He sank into the rocker. "Just like *Mamm* and *Daed* did."

Eli was struck speechless as Kyle rested one arm on the chair and wept. That his growing proficiency with reading lips would make his nephew feel abandoned had never crossed his mind. He'd thought Kyle had come to terms with Milan's and Shirley's deaths better than Eli had himself. The boy hadn't. He somehow had managed to hide his pain. Did Kyle believe as others did—including Eli—that his parents' deaths must be Eli's fault? Eli had dared to believe the boy didn't understand the depths of his guilt. Perhaps Kyle had been hiding that truth, too. A fresh flood of guilt washed over him until he felt as if he was going to drown.

"Are you okay?" Miriam mouthed, standing so Kyle couldn't read her lips.

He shook his head.

"Can I help?"

How he wanted to say *ja*! As he opened his mouth to release the truth he'd been withholding from her, the words wouldn't come. He couldn't bear the thought of her looking at him with disgust as he told her how he'd failed his brother. Others had done that, but others weren't the woman he was falling in love with.

He had to tell her. Just not when Kyle's pain seemed greater than his own.

"Help him," he said silently.

Miriam put her fingers on his arm and nodded.

Everything he'd said to the boy had been wrong. Maybe Miriam could do better. He prayed so. Once this crisis was past, he had to tell her the truth about the day Milan and Shirley had died. He trusted her with Kyle. Now he needed to trust her with the truth.

Miriam took a steadying breath. She couldn't let either Eli or Kyle down. Their bond, which had seemed unbreakable, was so fragile. They'd lost much the day Kyle's parents died. Severing the connection between them would be a tragedy, too.

She knelt by the little boy, but didn't touch him. "Kyle, Eli hasn't left you behind."

He didn't look at her. "He doesn't need my help anymore."

"Maybe not with understanding what others are saying, but he needs you in other ways. He's got this farm to take care of along with his carpentry work. Who helped him paint the chalkboard at school?"

"Me." The admission was reluctant.

"You help him in more ways than anyone can count."

"*Ja.* I help, but he doesn't need me."

She had to try something else before he stopped listening to her. "Kyle, look at me please."

Slowly, he did. His face was streaked with the trails of his tears.

"Eli does need you," she said, holding his gaze with her own. She chose every word with care, knowing the impact each could have. "Eli is here because of you. If you hadn't helped your *onkel* as you did, he might have given up."

"*Onkel* Eli doesn't give up." He glanced at Eli.

He put his hand on the boy's shoulder. "Miriam is right. Without your help, Kyle, I couldn't have imagined coming to Harmony Creek and joining this community. If you didn't help me practice, I wouldn't be able to read lips as well as I do."

"Is that true?"

As he gave his beloved nephew a gentle smile, he said, "I'll never lie to you, Kyle. No matter what happens, you can depend on me to be honest with you. There will be times when you may not like what I'm telling you. You might get angry or be sad, but you can be sure what I'm saying is the truth."

The *kind* said nothing for almost a full minute, then nodded. "So we are a team?"

"*Ja.*"

Kyle stood. "Can I have my sandwich and some new chips?"

Eli nodded. Kyle went into the kitchen and to the table. Once he was eating, Eli took Miriam's arm and steered her toward the front porch.

She went with him. No chairs offered a place to sit,

and he leaned one shoulder against an upright. She clasped her hands in front of her, feeling shy with him as she never had before. Easily she could have slipped into his arms.

"Danki," he said.

"For what?"

"For convincing Kyle that he and I are a team."

She smiled. "I was telling him what anyone can see. You two have become two parts of a whole."

"Hole?" Before she could answer, he gave her a wry grimace. "You mean whole as in complete, ain't so?"

"Ja. That's one of those words where you have to figure out what's being talked about by the context. It'll get easier with time."

"Or not, but I'm going to learn how to deal with it and not berate myself for not understanding everything the first time."

She took a step toward him. When he reached for her hands, she put them in his. She laced her fingers among his and gazed at his strong face that could be so tender.

"Do the same with Kyle," she said. "Learn how to deal with him and don't berate yourself if you don't understand him the first time." A giggle slipped past her lips. "And as soon as you learn something about him, he'll change. Keep telling him how important he is to you, so he knows it deep within his heart."

"As I should keep telling you how important you are to me?"

"Ja," she said as he drew her nearer. She rested her cheek against his chest and drank in the scents of his clothing. Her heart beat with the rhythm of his, and she couldn't imagine anywhere else she wanted to be.

He wasn't Yost. She could trust him to know she wanted the best for him and Kyle.

Couldn't she?

The first day back to school after the three-day holiday break was hot and humid. The *kinder* grew restless and had trouble concentrating on their lessons. In part, it was because they were in their new school building. The furniture had been moved in the afternoon before, and Miriam had spent an hour last night after supper hanging bright posters to add color to the white walls.

Deciding she was wasting her time—and the scholars'— by trying to teach them, she sent them outside for an early dismissal. Tomorrow, if the weather was fair, she would take them for a walk in the shady woods where they could learn about the variety of trees and look for signs of animals.

She glanced out the windows at where the scholars were playing softball. At the same time, she gathered the information she needed to write a final report on the impromptu school session. First, she compared what each *kind* had completed to the lessons in the syllabus. Almost all were ahead of where she'd prayed they'd be at this point.

God, danki *for putting a love of learning in their hearts*.

The Schmelley twins were the only ones lagging. She needed to talk to LaVon about them. In many ways the boys seemed younger than their six years. Many multiple births were complicated by the *bopplin* needing months in a hospital neonatal unit before coming home. A teacher she'd met in Lancaster had talked about being in a similar situation with her scholars. She said she'd read somewhere a *kind*'s age for judging skills, physical and mental, should be counted from the day he or she came home from the hospital, not the day they were born.

How long had the twins been in the hospital? With their *mamm* taking several weeks to recover from an infection, they probably had been kept longer than usual so LaVon could prepare himself for taking care of a sick wife and two newborns.

The twins had made enough progress, however, to satisfy the *Englisch* school superintendent. She bent to start writing the report she would give Caleb to deliver to Mr. Steele, who'd agreed, at long last, testing was unnecessary when school would be starting again in a few weeks. At that point the new teacher must begin keeping a record of the number of days school was held. That way if the *Englisch* district asked, the community could show they'd met the requirements of the state board of education.

Her pen faltered. A new teacher? Handing the job over to someone else was a sad thought, though Miriam had been so reluctant to take on the task of teaching a few weeks ago. She'd enjoyed her time with the scholars, and except for a couple of the boys who pushed her limits about the rule to stay in sight, the *kinder* had been well behaved. Eli had stopped checking on her to make sure she was keeping Kyle safe after school.

She could ask Caleb what he thought about her continuing on in the fall as the teacher. If he agreed that it was a *gut* idea, he then would speak on her behalf with the *daeds* who served as their school board and discover if they were interested in her keeping the job for a full year.

A flash of lightning brightened the school before vanishing. A thud of thunder swiftly followed. She glanced outside to see roiling clouds contorting in the sky. She hadn't noticed them building while working on the report. The storm was close, too close to let the scholars play ball or walk home along the tree-lined road.

Miriam half ran to the door and shouted for the *kinder* to come in at once. A gust of wind swept her words away. She picked up the bell by the door and rang it hard. As one, the scholars, who'd been so engrossed in their game they hadn't noticed the oncoming storm, either, whirled toward her. She motioned for them to hurry inside.

They ran toward her as another bolt struck somewhere farther south in the valley. Herding them through the door, she urged them not to stop to put the bats and balls away. That could wait until after the storm passed.

As she turned to tell them to take their seats, she gasped. Where was Kyle?

She didn't realize she'd spoken the words out loud until a boy said, "He went after the ball."

"Where?"

"It was hit into your yard. He went to get it."

Wishing this once Kyle hadn't offered to be so helpful, she strode to the door and opened it. She shouted his name over the rising wind, which whipped her skirt around her knees.

He must have heard her, because he paused and waved to her.

"Forget the ball!" she yelled and pointed at the darkening sky.

Looking in curiosity at the clouds, he didn't listen. Instead, he ran into the road just as a speeding car careened toward him.

Chapter Thirteen

The door crashed against the wall as Miriam rushed onto the school's porch. From the raised position, she could better see the car coming around the curve at a rapid speed. The driver wouldn't be able to see the boy until the last second. It'd be too late. He couldn't stop the car in time.

She called Kyle's name, but again, the wind stole her voice. Why had God sent a storm now?

She tried to run, but her legs felt like tree trunks, heavy and connected to the ground.

"Kyle!" she screamed, his name tearing out of her throat.

He turned in the middle of the road, staring at her in shock because she'd never raised her voice to the scholars before.

His motion and surprise freed her from her paralysis. She took several giant leaps forward, stretched out, grabbed his arm and yanked him back onto the grass. They fell to the ground as the car zipped by. It slowed for a second as if the driver was deciding whether to check if they were okay, then took off even faster.

The other *kinder* rushed from the building, alerted by her shriek.

Lifting the boy, Miriam ran to the school. She ordered the scholars inside. She held Kyle close as she followed them into the classroom. Was he trembling or was she? Maybe both at the thought of how close he'd come to being struck by the car.

She set him down, making sure he was steady before she released him. It took every bit of her flagging strength to tell him that they would collect the ball once the storm was past. Her knees barely held her as she walked to her desk and asked the scholars to sit at theirs. A sticky dampness on her right shin warned that she must have scraped it. She hoped she wouldn't bleed through her dark sock. That would upset the *kinder* more.

"Let's study our spelling words," she said as if nothing out of the ordinary had happened.

The scholars reached into their desks, then froze as lightning flashed and a gust of wind battered the school. The windows rattled again as the building shook with a rumble of thunder that exploded like the fireworks had on the Fourth of July.

It was followed by a louder crack. Through the windows on the right side of the school, she saw a tree shuddering by the road to her brother's farm. Suddenly, it toppled. *Kinder* shrieked, but their voices were muffled by the tree hitting the road so hard the branches bounced and slapped the asphalt a second time. Many shattered and were tossed by the wind toward the school.

"Stay in your seats," she ordered when several of the youngsters stood. She started to add more, but a motion on the other side of the school caught her eye.

Who was out in the rising storm? Had whoever it was lost his or her mind?

Before she could go to the door, it opened. Eli blew in along with leaves and broken twigs.

"Get away from the windows!" He hurried to each group of *kinder* and pulled them into the center of the room. "The wind is getting worse by the minute. We need to find shelter. Right away!"

When Miriam blanched, Eli knew she understood the severity of the storm surging into the hollow. The mountains that protected the valley from the most vicious storms had captured one and weren't letting it escape. He'd seen a few tornadoes in Delaware, and the damage they'd done had been horrific.

Were there tornadoes in northern New York in July? He had to assume it was possible. Even if the storm didn't get that bad, the furious winds were going to cause destruction.

"Shelter?" asked Miriam. "Where? Hiding under the desks won't make them any safer if a window shatters."

Wind slammed into the school again as if to emphasize her words.

"We can't get to the house," Eli said, though even the youngest *kind* must know that. "And we're too exposed in the school with so many windows. We'll have to ride out the storm in the storage closet."

"Impossible."

"There's plenty of room."

She shook her head. "It's filled with books and supplies for the fall."

"We need to clear it out." Yanking the closet door open, he wanted to groan. The space that had seemed so spacious when he'd been building it was now crammed with boxes.

He grabbed the first one and shoved it into her hands. She passed it along to one of the older *kinder* as she told the younger scholars to push the boxes out of the way. As the storm moved closer, he motioned the youngsters aside and set the boxes wherever he could reach. Miriam shifted them into haphazard piles, so he could keep pulling more out of the closet.

It felt like hours, but it couldn't have been more than three minutes before the closet was empty. As he stepped back from the doorway, Miriam sent each small *kind* in with a bigger scholar. Not one complained when she told them to hold on to each other as they squeezed into any available space. In the light of the nearly constant lightning flashes, their faces were bright with terror.

As soon as the *kinder* were inside, Eli asked, "What are you waiting for, Miriam? Get in!"

"Only if you do."

"Trust me. I will!" Putting his hand at the small of her back, he steered her into the closet.

She fit, but he wasn't sure if he would. When she reached past him and grabbed the door, pulling closed, he heard the *kinder* gasp as they were pressed more closely together.

"It'll pass soon," he called over the screeching wind. "Then we can unpack ourselves."

He couldn't tell if they heard him. Two of the youngest *kinder* were crying, hiding their faces against older scholars. Kyle, near the back, looked scared. Once the storm finished funneling down the creek, Eli would console him.

The door jerked from his hand. He grabbed for the

knob and missed. Wind swirled in, as if trying to sweep them out like a broom finding dust bunnies beneath a bed. He saw papers flying about the schoolroom. Had a window broken? An outer door blown open?

He didn't wait to find out. He pulled the door closed and locked his hands around the knob. It fought to escape him.

Would the building hold together?

Dear God, let it withstand the storm.

If it failed—as the wall on Milan's farm had failed—he would be to blame for every injury or worse that happened. Just as he'd been when his brother and sister-in-law had been crushed because of whatever mistake he'd made.

But he'd been extra careful with the construction of the school. Putting in more nails and supports than were necessary, wanting to guarantee nothing would cause the building to collapse. He'd done everything he could and more, but what if it wasn't enough?

A shiver ran along him. It wasn't his place to guarantee anything. It was God's. Though he had faith God had guided his hands and his decisions during the building of the school, the final outcome was known only to God.

When a slender arm encircled his shoulders, he realized the shifting *kinder* had brought Miriam to stand right next to him. She held Kyle and two other smaller scholars tight against her other side. He took one hand off the door, and his arm went around her waist, holding her to him. If these were to be his final moments, he wanted them to be with her.

"We'll be fine," she said, gazing at him so he couldn't miss the words her lips formed. "You built the school. We'll be safe here."

He expected her to add an "ain't so." She didn't, and when he met her earnest gaze, he saw she believed each word as if it were engraved in stone. For her to have such faith in him...

He didn't deserve it, but he craved it. If she believed in him, maybe—just maybe—he could begin to believe in himself again.

No! That would lead to the same arrogance that caused him to ignore the mistakes in the wall's construction.

Something struck the school. Everything shook. There was a scream even he could hear, but he wasn't sure if it was the wind or the *kinder*.

He grasped Kyle by the sleeve and yelled for the scholars to hold onto each other. He doubted that would help if a twister was ready to pull the school apart.

Then the only sound was rain. Had the storm moved on, or was it a lull?

Everyone seemed to be holding their breaths and straining to hear what was going on beyond the closet. When he looked at Miriam, she nodded in response to his unspoken question.

He pushed the door open and stepped out. Papers crackled beneath his feet. Every surface in the room was covered in a thin layer of white. The chalkboard was plastered with papers. The whiteboard Miriam had brought to the school had been tipped over, markers strewn everywhere. He wondered how long it would take to sort out everything.

But at least the scholars hadn't been tossed around, too.

Eli went to the back door. It was ajar and rocked in the remnants of the wind. He closed and latched it. The windows were intact, though they were so covered with bits of green it was impossible to see through them. The front door had withstood the storm.

Miriam led the *kinder* from the closet while Eli went outside. She urged them to thank God for bringing them through safely. Saying his own grateful prayer, Eli looked around.

A big branch had hit the porch and was shattered into pieces no bigger than matchsticks. One of the porch railing posts was cracked. Otherwise, the rail was secure. Two boards flapped at one side of the building. The corner piece holding them in place must have been torn off.

"The school rode out the storm well," said Caleb when he arrived and picked his way through the downed branches. "If you hadn't insisted on those extra nails in the roof boards, the whole roof might have been ripped off."

"I wanted to keep the *kinder safe*."

Caleb clapped him on the shoulder. "The *kinder* and their teacher, ain't so?"

"When I worked on it, I hoped, as the rest of the builders did, anyone who enters the schoolhouse will be safe," he said, acting as if he didn't understand what the other man was saying.

That was the last chance Eli had for conversation the rest of the day. While parents came to collect the scholars and see them home, many returning to help clean up, he listened to reports of damage. Shingles had been torn off, and another tree blocked the road in front of the empty house next door to the Waglers' farm. The faint sound of a chain saw announced someone was at work removing it.

A large Town of Salem truck stopped beside the tree in the road between the school and Miriam's house.

Four men and two more chain saws were soon cutting the giant tree into smaller pieces and stacking them in front of the school. The supervisor said they'd return to collect the wood, but Caleb told them that wasn't necessary. The Kuhns brothers would drag it to their sawmill. The *Englischer* smiled, relieved, that was one task he could strike off his long to-do list. The storm hadn't spared any section of town. The *gut* news was nobody had been gravely hurt.

Eli tossed a branch on the tall pile behind the stack of wood. The smaller ones and leaves would have to be raked. The scholars could do that in the morning when the grass was drier.

A plastic glass of lemonade was held out to him, and he seized it, downing the contents before he realized Miriam had handed it to him. She filled the glass again from the pitcher she carried along with a tower of glasses. Before he could thank her, she rushed to offer someone else a refreshing drink. She flitted from one person to the next like a busy bee in a field of flowers.

He sipped to make the lemonade last longer and sat on the school's porch by the steps. He'd replace the cracked rail tomorrow before he went back to work shoring up the Osbornes' sunporch.

When Kyle plopped down beside him, Eli ruffled his nephew's hair. "Pretty exciting day at school today, ain't so?"

"Ja." He took a deep drink of his own lemonade, then jumped to his feet as Miriam walked toward them.

Eli noticed dried blood on one of her black socks. Had she hurt herself while clearing away the mess in the schoolyard?

Kyle paid no attention. He started to give her a hug,

but she waved him back with a smile until she'd put the pitcher and remaining glasses on the porch.

She held out her arms, and Kyle threw herself into them. Over the *kind*'s head, she smiled at Eli.

"I was saying to Kyle," Eli said as he stood, "that it was an exciting day at school."

"Too exciting," she replied. "I'm so glad you were here to help with the *kinder*."

"You could have saved them by yourself."

"I would like to think so, but…"

Kyle interjected, "You would have, Miriam. You saved me *twice* today."

"Twice?" Eli asked.

Miriam started to reply, but the excited boy burst in and told how, when he'd gone to retrieve the ball, she'd pulled him out of the road before a car could run him over.

With every word, anger rose in Eli. He'd listened to Miriam's reassurance his nephew would be safe, and she'd let him run into the road when a car was barreling toward him.

Kyle wasn't finished with his tale, but Eli interrupted to demand, "Why weren't you watching him, Miriam? He could have been killed. I thought I could trust you to protect him. You didn't!"

Her face had become a sickly gray. She lowered her eyes.

"She did!" Kyle stamped his foot so hard the boards reverberated beneath Eli's boots. The boy yanked on his sleeve and threads snapped. "*I* went after the ball. Miriam called to me to come inside, but I didn't listen to her. I kept going after the ball. It's my fault. Not hers."

A rational part of Eli's mind urged him to listen

to Kyle. Instead, he grabbed the little boy's hand and strode down the steps. He looked at Miriam. She hadn't moved.

She must regret not keeping better track of the boy. But the thought of what could have happened, how he could have lost the last member of his family, ached inside him. It laid another thick layer of guilt to silence his foolish heart that told him he hadn't been wrong to trust again or to love again when he'd thought it would be impossible to find someone who would accept both him and Kyle.

The boy protested as Eli steered him toward the buggy. No matter what his nephew said, Eli must not do anything to risk the *kind* again. Dissolving into angry tears as they drove away, Kyle didn't look at him.

And Eli didn't look back.

Chapter Fourteen

Eli slowed his buggy in front of the school on the last day of school. His nephew slid out and loped toward the building, not waving goodbye as he used to.

"Kyle?" Eli called.

Reluctantly, the boy stopped. Eli thought he wouldn't face him, but Kyle did, his right hand in his pocket. His expression wavered between hurt and anger. He'd worn that expression for the past week since he'd admitted the day after the storm that he feared his *onkel* would pull him out of school.

Eli had considered it, but the trouble that could cause the settlement had halted him. And what would he have done with his nephew while he was rebuilding the Osbornes' sunporch? The boy was helpful on a job site, but Eli wasn't sure how *Englischers* would feel about a *kind* there. It was important to get this first job right, so others would offer him work.

"Don't forget," Eli said. "I'll pick you up after I get done with my meeting this afternoon."

"I know." Kyle's tone was petulant.

"Don't head home by yourself and no ball games."

"I know." The boy's shoulders hunched, and he stuck his other hand in a pocket, too. It was as if he'd grown into a rebellious teen in the blink of an eye.

Then Kyle spun and ran toward the school.

Sighing, Eli rested his elbows on his knees. How could life turn from *gut* to horrible this fast?

His mind was mired in exhaustion. He hadn't slept much for the past four nights, thinking of how he'd reacted to the news a car had nearly run over his nephew.

Or, according to Kyle, how he'd overreacted.

Kyle was so furious with him that for a day, he'd refused to look at Eli while speaking. Eli had insisted, and the boy obeyed, but hadn't said much other than to repeat Miriam had done nothing wrong. She'd saved his life. Hadn't Eli noticed the blood on her leg? Kyle was sure that had happened when she risked herself to pull him out of the road.

Eli had seen the blood on her black sock, but she wouldn't have been hurt if she'd been keeping a closer eye on a rambunctious boy. He wanted to believe Kyle, but his nephew was a *kind*. He didn't understand that in spite of Miriam saving him, she'd allowed her attention to be drawn away in the first place.

His nephew didn't know how Eli had made a promise by his brother's casket to keep the boy safe. If Eli had done that instead of letting Miriam persuade him to go against his best instincts, nothing would have happened.

He couldn't explain to Kyle that he was angrier at himself than he was at either Miriam or the boy. He'd been shown what could happen if he forgot his promise…even once.

The school door opened as Kyle reached it. When Miriam stepped out, Eli's breath caught in his throat.

His arms could almost feel her soft curves in them. She didn't move as the distance between them dissolved until he could almost believe that if he reached out, he could take her hand. And he wanted to. He ached to pull her close and breathe in the fresh scent of her hair and savor her fingers' light caress as they uncurled along his face or wove through his own fingers.

His heart urged him to go to her, to tell her that he didn't want what they shared to come to an end like this. To tell her that he loved her as he had no other woman. As he would never love another woman.

But his duty to his late brother halted him. He'd never guessed a pledge made in *gut* faith could destroy his hopes for love.

As soon as Miriam said the day was over, the scholars rushed toward the door. The enthusiasm that had been with them at the beginning of their unplanned term was gone. In the aftermath of the big storm, the air had been wiped clean of humidity. The *kinder* wanted to be outside, enjoying the freshness.

The special school session was finished.

Just like any dreams she'd had about her and Eli. Those were gone almost before they'd begun.

Should she have defended herself when Eli accused her of being careless? How could she have done that when Eli was right? She should have kept a closer eye on Kyle. She'd said she would, and then she had let herself become distracted...as she had the day Ralph had almost drowned.

In each case the boys had survived thanks to her, but they shouldn't have been in such dangerous circumstances to begin with. She closed the door and walked to her desk to finish the report on the term. It was just as well she hadn't spoken with Caleb about applying to teach during the new school year.

Her breath hitched as she sat and stared at the page. The words blurred. What would she do with the rest of her life?

She looked at the small package on the desk. She'd offered to take it to the post office after school because Caleb had a long day in the fields and planned to meet with the other men after supper to discuss the clothing issues they needed to define for their *Ordnung*. Running errands was something she could do to help, but eventually Caleb would marry, and he'd have someone else to oversee his household. Where would Miriam live then? Maybe one or more of the other members of the Spinsters' Club would find a small house somewhere to live together.

The jesting name no longer seemed funny. It sounded lonely.

"Miriam?"

Surprised by Kyle's voice, she looked up from her clasped hands on the desk. She'd assumed he'd left with the other *kinder*.

Again, she'd failed to keep track of the boy. In spite of her broken heart, she hadn't learned a thing.

She stopped rebuking herself when she met Kyle's eyes. They were dull with unhappiness, and hints of red suggested the little boy had been crying. She hadn't seen any tears on his face while the scholars were inside, but she thought about how, after the *kinder* were released, he hadn't joined in the last game before their shortened vacation. He'd been standing by the tree with

Mercy's son Paul. She'd seen Paul pat Kyle on the shoulder. Had the little boy been crying then?

Her heart threatened to break anew. She stood and walked around her desk. Taking his trembling hand, she led him to a desk. He sat at it, and she pulled out the chair of the next one.

Lowering herself to the tiny seat, she asked, "Is Eli coming to get you, Kyle?"

"Ja."

"At Paul's house?" The two boys had walked there after school each day since the storm. They left right after school was out, not staying to play ball.

"Paul has something he has to do this afternoon, so I decided to stay here with you, which is *gut* because I want to—that is, I need to…" A flush climbed his face.

"Do you want to talk to me about something, Kyle?"

He nodded, drawing his lower lip beneath his one upper tooth that hadn't fallen out yet.

"Go ahead," she urged.

He opened his mouth but clamped it closed again as if he didn't dare to let words escape. As if he was frightened by the strength of his own emotions.

Ach, how she wanted to draw him into her arms and tell him she shared his dread. Every word she'd said since the day of the storm had been the wrong one. Either an evasion from the truth or an attempt to deny what she felt. She avoided any conversation that might turn to her and Eli and how she'd failed him. Her brother and the members of the Spinsters' Club were giving her time to tell them what was bothering her in the wake of the tempest, but she wasn't sure how long their patience would hold up.

"Sometimes it's hard to say what is inside of us,

ain't so?" She had to stop fretting over her own problems and help the *kind*, if she could, with whatever was bothering him.

He nodded, staring at the toes of his scuffed shoes as he swung his feet against the chair legs.

She leaned forward to where she could catch his eyes. "When I find it hard to say what I'm feeling, I know there's only one thing to do. I have to say it. Once I do, I feel better."

"Really?"

"Ja," she replied, but glanced toward the door as if she'd heard someone outside.

She couldn't meet the little boy's eyes any longer. Would he see how guilty she felt about giving advice she hadn't taken for herself? Or was she seeking a bit of his courage to enable herself to face the truth that she'd destroyed any affection Eli might have had for her? Not that she could blame him. Yost had acted the same way when she messed up. But she had been sure she'd learned her lesson and would be extra careful with *kinder*, particularly with mischievous little boys. Maybe she had, but not well enough.

"Miriam?"

Again, his tiny voice, barely more than a whisper, shredded her thoughts.

"Ja?" she prompted.

"Why is *Onkel* Eli mad at me?"

She smiled gently at him. "He's not angry with you. He's angry with me."

"He *is* mad at you," Kyle asserted, "but he's mad at me, too."

"Why do you think that?"

"He's acting strange."

"Maybe he has something on his mind." *Something like how disappointed he is in me.*

The boy shook his head with the certainty of a six-year-old. "He's had stuff on his mind before, and he never acted like this. He has a hard time hearing, but he used to be *gut* at listening. He hasn't been listening to me—really listening—since we've moved here." He propped his elbow on the desk and his chin on his palm.

"I'm sure he's listening to you the best he can." She was surprised how right it felt to defend Eli, though he hadn't given her much of a chance to explain what had happened the day of the storm. What could she have said? That she'd made the same mistake of trusting a *kind* who had his mind set on a course of action? "Remember? He has to concentrate on reading lips. It isn't easy for him."

"No, he isn't listening!" Kyle gave her a frown, which made him look more like his *onkel* than ever. "Will *you* please listen to me, Miriam? *Onkel* Eli thinks I'm upset with him."

"For what?"

"For selling my *daed*'s farm."

Miriam hesitated. If she said the wrong thing, she could cause more damage. "Why do you think that?" she asked, deciding to let the little boy lead the conversation that was going in a very unexpected direction.

"I heard talk back in Delaware about what a shame it was *Onkel* Eli got rid of the farm when families in our district had to move out because there aren't farms available." His forehead ruffled with his puzzled expression. "I didn't understand that because he sold it to the son of one of our plain neighbors."

Little pitchers have big ears.

She suspected the little boy had misconstrued the conversation, but she didn't want to complicate matters by saying that. Instead, she patted Kyle's shoulder as he leaned his chin on his hand again. "You know there's an easy way to clear this up, don't you?"

"*Ja*. If I give *Onkel* Eli a gift, he won't be angry with me anymore."

"You don't need to get him a gift. He knows how much you care about him."

He shook his head. "I'm not sure if he does, but he'll believe me when I give him something I know he wants. After he's happy with my gift, I can tell him that I know he sold my *daed*'s farm because he wanted the two of us to have a new and better life here." He rubbed a knuckle against his eye, but tears welled out and trickled down his round cheek. "He thinks he's hiding it, but he's sad about the day *Mamm* and *Daed* died." His mouth tightened. "He believes the accident when the wall collapsed on them was his fault."

"Why would he think that?" she blurted.

The boy had to have misheard again. She didn't—couldn't—accept that Eli had had anything to do with the tragedy other than as a victim. He was the most cautious person she'd ever met, watching out for any possible contingency that would be dangerous. His work on the school had saved them from being hurt in the storm. He watched over Kyle, almost stifling the little boy. How could anyone so careful imperil his family?

Or, her mind argued, *is he anxious because of the error he made four years ago?* He battled a deep-seated pain. Because of his failure to see the wall was unsteady before it toppled?

"*Onkel* Eli believed what was said by people who were mean to him at the funeral."

"Weren't you too young to remember it?"

"I remember bits. How everyone was sad. How it was a sunny day, but then there was a thunderstorm. I also remember hearing people say those mean people who blamed *Onkel* Eli were *Mamm*'s cousins. They said her cousins needed to be forgiven because they'd lashed out in pain. What does that mean?"

How often had Eli's neighbors spoken bluntly because they knew he wouldn't hear what they were talking about? They'd failed to realize Kyle was standing there, soaking up everything they'd said.

"It means," she said to answer his question, "those people said things they shouldn't have. That their grief kept them from thinking straight or knowing their words would have painful repercussions."

Pride slipped into his voice. "*Onkel* Eli turned the other cheek as Jesus said we're supposed to. He refused to argue with them." His shoulders slumped. "But he believes they were right. Others—a lot of others—didn't believe the wall falling was *Onkel* Eli's fault. Maybe he didn't hear what our neighbors kept saying."

Miriam had grown numb with shock as Kyle's explanation added layer after layer of additional heartache for Eli. She must say something. The boy was looking at her, hoping she'd confirm his words, though she'd never met any of the people he was referring to.

"It's likely he didn't hear your neighbors," she said, responding to the most innocuous thing Kyle had said. "You know as well as I do your *onkel* missed a lot of what was being said around him before he began to read lips." Again, she spoke with care, not wanting to cause Kyle distress at the reminder of how independent Eli could be.

"I wish he'd learned a long time ago."

She felt her own shoulders ease a bit at the boy's words. He'd set aside his hurt at not being indispensable to his *onkel*.

But could it be true Eli's inattention to the wall-building project had led to the disaster? She stiffened again. From the first day she'd met Eli, she'd sensed he was carrying a heavy burden. For him to believe he'd caused the deaths of two people who were so important to him would place an unbearable weight upon his soul. No wonder he yearned to shield Kyle from even a faintest hint of danger.

Unaware of her thoughts, the youngster went on, "Some folks said it was *Onkel* Eli's fault, because he was the one who knows construction and should have seen the problem before the wall fell. Others insisted my *daed* must have made a mistake somewhere along the way and hid it from *Onkel* Eli. Our bishop warned folks to keep their opinions to themselves because the only One who knew the truth was God." Kyle looked at her with wet eyes. "The bishop wouldn't have said it if it wasn't so, ain't so?"

Again, she didn't answer right away. When he began to squirm in the seat, she said, "It's true God knows every event in our lives and every thought in our heads and every beat of our hearts. Bishops are honest, just as they ask us to be when they urge us to tell the truth, and we try, but sometimes it's not easy."

"I know, but some people seem to like lies better than the truth."

"Maybe they don't know what they're saying isn't true."

Kyle stuck out his chin in an obstinate frown. "They had to know *Onkel* Eli wouldn't do anything to hurt someone else."

"Of course he wouldn't."

Tears rushed into her eyes, and she turned away before Kyle could see them. The boy was upset. He didn't need to have her pain added to his. She'd thought he was oblivious to the real reasons his *onkel* had insisted he no longer stay after school, but Kyle had known better than she had.

Her first instinct was to sit on the porch and wait for Eli to arrive. Would he listen to her when she told him how sorry she was for his pain, or would he refuse to acknowledge her sympathy and forgiveness? Would he walk away…for *gut* this time?

That Eli had dared to trust her showed the depth of his feelings for her, because he didn't trust anyone else, not even himself. And she'd let him down, as she had Yost.

But it was different. Yost had been growing distant in their last few weeks as a betrothed couple. When he'd come to the house, there had been undeniable tension in the air. Not just between Yost and her, but between her betrothed and Caleb. Her brother had refused to explain why he didn't want to be in the same room with the man she planned to marry. Though Caleb had comforted her, she'd sensed his relief that she would never be Yost's wife.

She hadn't ever figured out why the onetime friendship between Caleb and Yost had soured. She must have been too focused on spending time with Ralph to see what had happened. Or had she been like Kyle, witnessing exchanges she somehow couldn't understand because she didn't have the facts and attempted to fill in the blanks herself?

Not once had she defended herself against Yost's accusations. She couldn't imagine Eli doing such a thing; yet his silence was worse. She had to think of a way to ask how she could regain his trust.

"Will you take me today?" Kyle asked.

Miriam blinked as if waking from a deep sleep. "Take you? Where?"

"Will you take me to the hardware store?" Impatience laced through his voice.

"Why do you need to go to the hardware store today?"

He stood and regarded her with an expression that conveyed without words that he was wondering if she'd lost her mind. "I told you. I want to get *Onkel* Eli a gift, so he knows I'm not mad at him. They've got a hammer there that I know he'd like to have." Reaching into his pocket, he pulled out a small plastic bag filled with coins and a collection of glass marbles. "Won't you help me buy him a gift to make him be happy again?"

Her gaze cut to Caleb's package on the desk. If she waited for Eli to finish his day's work and return to Harmony Creek, she wouldn't get to the post office before it closed. She had to go into Salem, but she couldn't leave the little boy by himself at the school.

"Okay," she said, "but we must leave a note for your *onkel*."

His brow furrowed, and she thought he'd protest. Then he nodded with a grin.

Miriam wrote a quick note on the whiteboard in blue

marker. It let Eli know that Kyle was with her and they'd gone into town. Eli was sure to notice the bright blue letters when he walked into the school to look for his nephew.

"Let's go," she said. "We need to be quick, so we're back before your *onkel* gets here." She held out her hand, and he took it.

As they went down the steps, Kyle gasped. "I forgot my money!"

She sent him to get it while she hitched the horse to the buggy. Kyle ran into the schoolhouse and returned wearing an even bigger grin. He grabbed her hand and talked on and on about how *wunderbaar* it was going to be to give Eli a special surprise. How it was going to make everything all right again.

She wished she had his faith that a heartfelt effort would close the chasm between Eli and his nephew. If she did, maybe she could find a way to do the same for her and Eli. Maybe it was still possible to return to the time when being in each other's arms was the most important thing in the world.

Chapter Fifteen

"**D**o you know where the hammer you want is?" Miriam asked as she opened the door to the hardware store on Main Street. The cool dusk inside was a welcome relief from the bright sunshine making shimmering waves along the sidewalk. Steam rose from the hot concrete. The sprinkle that had fallen on their way into the village hadn't relieved the humidity. Rather, the air seemed heavier than before the spotty rain.

She needed to hurry Kyle because she'd left in the buggy the few groceries she'd bought after stopping at the post office. The buggy was parked in front of the grocery store at the only hitching rail in the village. One was planned near the library, but the work hadn't been completed.

Not that she would have used it because the grocery store was closer to the hardware store. More dark clouds were gathering in the northwest corner of the sky, so they needed to finish their errands and get home before the storm broke.

Kyle had been eyeing the clouds, and she was sure he was thinking—as she was—about the tempest that had swept over the school. But he wouldn't be remembering Eli's strong arms holding her close as he protected her and comforted her. The memory was bittersweet, but she couldn't change what had happened after she'd believed the worst of the storm had passed.

"*Ja*, I know where the hammer is." Kyle called a greeting to Tuck, the man behind the counter.

She guessed Tuck was the owner, so she returned his smile.

Kyle didn't give her a chance to say anything. He was almost hopping in his excitement at buying a gift for his *onkel*. He'd been as patient as possible while they stood behind two other customers at the post office and then went to the grocery store. He couldn't wait a second longer.

Taking her hand, he led her around bins and racks of items for sale to what must have at one time been a separate store because there was a door to the street in the other half of the store. Three lawn mowers and a snowblower blocked it. Two tents, one put together, were set in front of the machines. She wondered how long it'd been since that door was opened.

She slowed herself and Kyle before they could run into an *Englischer*. The dark-haired man who wore denim overalls stepped aside, dropping a roll of chicken wire.

"Excuse us," she said.

He nodded and smiled as Kyle slipped past him and continued toward where the hammer he wanted was waiting. "Someone's in a big hurry, isn't he?"

"He is."

"Boys at that age seem to have two speeds. Fast and faster."

Glad the *Englischer* was kind, she gave him room to pass with the chicken wire before saying in *Deitsch*, "Kyle, apologize please."

Kyle did as the man walked toward a long counter with a modern register at one end. Then the boy focused on a pegboard where hand tools were displayed. There were more varieties of screwdrivers than Miriam had guessed existed. Manual ones and battery-operated ones and electric ones. Fortunately, there were fewer choices for the hammers.

"Which one?" she asked.

"That one! Right there!" He looked at her with a smile that revealed his lone top front tooth was getting loose enough to hang at an angle.

She reached for one with a black handle, but he shook his head.

"The one beside it," he said. "The green one."

She smiled as she lifted the hammer he wanted from the display. She handed it to him and watched as he examined it.

For a very short moment, she'd dared to dream this sweet little boy would become her son when she married the man raising him. A man she was ready to give her heart to for the rest of her life. Once again her hopes had been foolish. More foolish than in Lancaster County. At least then Yost had asked her to marry him. Eli had said nothing of them having a future together.

"Do you think *Onkel* Eli will like it?" Kyle asked.

"I'm sure he will because you got it for him." The words were automatic, and she scolded herself for putting her own sorrow before his excitement.

"Maybe he'll let me use it sometimes."

"Maybe."

She glanced over her shoulder as the front door opened. Two men walked in, but moved to a different section of the store. She put out her hand to make sure Kyle didn't take it into his head to go and see what they were doing and almost run into them, too.

"Let's pay for this," she said. "I want to get back before we end up soaked."

He held out his bag of change. "I've got eight dollars and forty-three cents. That's enough, ain't so?"

Looking at the board where the prices were listed, she nodded, though he was a couple of dollars short. She hoped she could slip the store owner the extra money without Kyle noticing. The boy was staring at the hammer, fascinated, so it shouldn't be hard to make up the difference. She could always ask Kyle to separate his money from his marbles. That would keep him from seeing her add to his total.

"It'll be fine." She smiled at him, admitting to herself she hoped the gift would persuade Eli to listen to her as well as to Kyle.

She whirled at the sound of a bitten-off curse and a shriek. Glancing toward the door, she saw a silhouette vanish out the front door into the eye-searing sunshine. She noticed that before her eyes focused on two men by the counter. One wore a black ski mask, the other, shorter by almost a head, wore a bright green one with a garish face on it.

Something glinted in one man's hand.

"He's got a gun," Kyle moaned beside her, clutching her skirt in terror.

"Don't anyone else move!" snarled a man whose voice was higher pitched than Tuck's. "This is a robbery!"

"What do we do?" Kyle whispered.

Pulling him to her, she answered, "Don't move and pray hard. Harder than you ever have."

Eli strode past a field where beef cattle grazed in complete indifference to the storm coming toward the hollow. A pile of sawdust had grown into a mound beside the busy sawmill.

The Kuhns brothers had set up the mill in an open-sided building near the woods behind their barn. Instead of tending to a crop in the fields, they were using the summer to cut lumber from the trees they'd felled in the woods higher on the hillside. In the winter they planned to sell Christmas trees from the lot that had been on their farm when they bought it. The Amish didn't put trees in their houses and decorate them, but selling them would help the family make a success of the farm.

Stone ridges cut through most of the fields, so they weren't good for much but grazing and lumber. He'd heard the brothers were thinking of starting an apple orchard, but the trees needed to grow between three and five years—depending on what variety the brothers planted—before bearing fruit. The Christmas trees, meanwhile, would provide a comfortable income for the family.

Eli winced and covered his ears as he walked into the open-sided building. The shriek of steel and belts as the saw sliced through an oak log was blistering when augmented by his hearing aids. He turned them down before he took another step. It shouldn't take him long to get the boards he needed to finish the Osborne project and to start his next one.

He smiled. The job offer had come less than two hours ago, an *Englischer* who lived a few doors away from the Osbornes. It was a bigger project, a complete kitchen renovation. He wanted to bring Jeremiah Stoltzfus in on the project, because the *Englischer* had talked about having a corner table with raw edges to match the rustic decor they were planning for the whole house. That would require a skilled woodworker like Jeremiah.

His smile broadened when he saw Jeremiah standing with three other men by the saw. Jeremiah was examining a length of wood that had been sliced off a log. It was thick enough for a tabletop, so Eli guessed his neighbor would soon be shaping it into one of the beautiful pieces of furniture that had caught the attention of *Englischers*. Rumor suggested more than one interior decorator from New York City had traveled almost two hundred miles north to arrange for Jeremiah to make furniture for picky clients in the city. No wonder the man who'd hired Eli had been so pleased when he'd mentioned the idea of having Jeremiah contribute to the kitchen project.

The men yelled greetings before returning to their shouted conversation. Over and over as he walked toward them, he noticed how they asked whoever was speaking to repeat himself. Just as Miriam had told him, nobody seemed bothered by the request.

He could understand every word spoken. Being able to "hear" others when they couldn't hear him was bizarre. Miriam's lessons on lipreading and body language allowed him to understand what two men on the other side of the saw were discussing.

It took three tries before Jeremiah understood that

Eli wanted his assistance on a job in Salem. Smiling, Jeremiah agreed to go with him tomorrow and bring designs to share with his new clients.

Eli thanked him and turned to leave. He was late getting Kyle at the school. Knowing he should have stopped on his way to the sawmill, he realized he owed his nephew and Miriam an apology for being late.

And for so many other things.

After praying for God's guidance, he was trying to accept he couldn't change the past and letting it destroy his present and future was going against God's will. He owed forgiveness to so many, including those who had accused him of carelessness. He hoped Kyle would accept his apology for refusing to listen to the boy.

But most of all, he needed to ask Miriam to forgive him. Kyle had insisted she hadn't been to blame for his being almost hit by a car. She had saved him. Rather than listen to the facts, Eli had let past events propel him into making unfounded accusations. He didn't want to think of what would happen if she forgave him but wanted nothing more to do with him.

A hand grasped his arm. He looked over his shoulder to see Caleb behind him.

"Can we talk somewhere quiet?" Caleb bellowed.

Eli nodded and followed his friend out of the sawmill. Turning up his hearing aids once they'd put distance between them and the shrill machinery, Eli leaned one shoulder against a tree and waited while Caleb turned to face him.

"This isn't easy to say," Caleb said, rubbing his hands.

"Then spit it out and be done with it."

"*Ja*, that's *gut* advice." He met Eli's eyes. "Miriam

was upset after the storm. It wasn't the danger you'd faced. It was something much more painful to her. Do you know why?"

He wasn't going to lie. "I do."

"Will you tell me?"

"She didn't?"

Caleb shook his head. "Miriam is a private person at the best of times. When she's upset, she becomes more closed. You may have noticed that."

"I have."

"What happened?"

It didn't take Eli long to explain, saying nothing to excuse his part in what had occurred.

With each word spoken, Caleb's face crumbled more. He shook his head and sighed. Not that Eli could hear the sound, but he recognized the rise and fall of Caleb's shoulders.

"I was afraid something like that had happened," Caleb said. "No wonder she was so shattered."

"We've had differences of opinion before, but she never reacted as she did then."

"I'm sure she didn't." Caleb gnawed on his bottom lip, and Eli could see he was debating with himself. "What I'm about to tell you can't go any further."

"Gossiping isn't something I do, even when I could hear well."

"*Gut*, because what I've got to tell you isn't something that should be spread around. Miriam has already had to deal with half-truths and outright lies spoken by people who should know better." Taking a deep breath, he said, "Before we moved to this settlement, Miriam was set to be married."

"She was?" Eli was stunned. Not once had she given him any hint she'd been serious about a man in the past.

"To a widowed neighbor of ours. Yost Fisher. I was surprised when she told me that they were planning to marry. I thought Miriam could see he was only looking for someone to oversee his house and take care of his son, nothing more."

"Love is blind, so they say."

"And they are right." Caleb gave him a crooked grin. "Miriam was in love. Not with Yost, but with his six-year-old son, Ralph. The two of them seemed to be meant to be together. That was why I urged her to take the teaching job for the summer. She loves being with *kinder.*"

"They adore her, too." He thought of how his nephew looked for any excuse to spend time with Miriam. Even when he was supposed to be playing with friends, he sought her out. "Why did she seem hesitant about taking over the school for the summer?"

"Because Ralph nearly drowned. Miriam saved his life."

"Thank God He put her in the right place to help the boy. But what does that have to do with her being unsure about being around kids?"

"The boy's *daed* blamed her for the boy getting into trouble in the first place." Caleb's mouth tightened into a thin line. "Yost, who should have been keeping an eye on the boy, was, as I learned later, with another woman several districts from where we lived."

"What?"

"He'd been seeing her for quite a while. He left his son with Miriam when he had to go away on what he called *business.*"

"But he was spending time with this other woman."

Caleb nodded. "Miriam never found out about what Yost had been doing. He made sure of that by proclaiming it was Miriam's fault for what happened to the boy instead of being grateful. He never took an ounce of blame himself because he didn't bother to make sure Ralph got to our house. How could he...?"

Eli hung his head. He didn't need to see Caleb's expression to know he'd be a hypocrite if he condemned Yost Fisher. Like the man he'd never met, he'd accused Miriam of endangering a *kind* when, instead, she'd kept Kyle from being hurt.

Fingers tapped on his arm, and he looked up.

"Miriam said you can't hear everything," Caleb said, his face taut with distress, "unless you're looking at the person talking."

"True."

The other man had more to say, and he didn't intend for Eli to miss a single word. "You've got to understand, Eli. What Yost did broke her heart...and her spirit. I wasn't sure if she'd heal." He gave a terse laugh. "She wouldn't have if she remained behind when I came here. People who should have known she'd never do anything to endanger a *kind* started to believe, when she didn't defend herself, that maybe Yost was right."

"Did you?"

"No." His smile was sad as his gaze turned inward with memories of what must have been a terrible time for the whole Hartz family. "But I know Miriam always would wonder. That's why I asked her to be the teacher for our summer school."

"So you devised the plan for having the scholars return to school?"

Caleb shook his head. "No, that wasn't my doing. The minimum days of school had to be taken care of, but as soon as I heard that, I jumped at the chance to show my sister that we trusted her with the *kinder*. She'd started to believe it again."

"Until I accused her of not watching over Kyle and the other scholars as I believed she should have." He didn't make it a question. He and Caleb knew it was the truth. "Even if she'd been watching the scholars every second, she still wouldn't have stopped Kyle from going to get the ball. She tried, and he didn't listen. She did all she promised to do." His voice broke in his throat. "And she saved his life. I let my fear for him make me do the stupidest thing I could have."

Pushing off the tree, Eli left without saying where he was going. Caleb knew, too, that it was long past time for Eli to tell Miriam he'd made a big mistake and he was sorry.

But an hour later he still hadn't had a chance to apologize. She wasn't at home nor at the school, though he guessed she'd been earlier because a quartet of colorful posters had been rehung around the room. Kyle must have been with her then because Eli could see erased words on the whiteboard where his nephew liked to write, but the boy was gone, too. He hoped Kyle was with her.

As he drove toward his farm at the far end of the hollow, Eli stopped at the Waglers' farm. Neither twin nor anyone else there had seen Miriam or Kyle that afternoon. He didn't bother to visit the Kuhnses' farm because Sarah wouldn't be home during the week.

Maybe Miriam had gone to visit her at the Summerhayses' house. Would she have taken Kyle with her? It was possible. Eli recalled there was at least one *kind* in Sarah's care who was about his nephew's age.

Turning around, he drove toward the main road. He saw Mercy waving to him as he passed her house. He slowed the buggy. Maybe Mercy had seen her and Kyle.

As the buggy rolled to a stop, he realized what a change Miriam had made in his life. He never would have, after the wall's collapse, considered instigating a conversation. Instead, he would have scurried away like a frightened woodchuck hurrying into its den.

Mercy came to the road. To his question, she nodded. "I saw her drive past about an hour ago. She had Kyle with her. They stopped, and said they were heading into town for an important errand." She smiled as she wiped her hands on her apron. "She said if I saw you to let you know that she'd left you a note at school."

He started to say he hadn't seen any note, then thought of the partial words on the whiteboard. Had it been the message left by Miriam? But if so, who had erased it?

Mercy tugged on his sleeve, and he looked at her. "Kyle had an errand at the hardware store today. She told me to tell you he'd explain when they got back."

"They went into the village?"

"As far as I know, *ja*."

"*Danki*, Mercy." He drove away slowly so he didn't raise a cloud of dust to choke her.

The creek road had never seemed so long, but when he got to the main road, he drew in his horse. Chasing her and Kyle into Salem was *dumm*. What was he going to do when he found them? *Ja*, he and Miriam needed to talk, but what he had to say to her he didn't want to say in the middle of a crowd of *Englischers*. Or among their Amish neighbors. The private conversation that was long overdue could wait until she returned home. He should head to Caleb's farm so he would be there when she and Kyle got back.

Hearing a rumble of thunder to the west confirmed his decision. Miriam would stay in Salem until after the storm was over. He'd be a *dummkopf* to continue to town while he and his horse got soaked. Another glance at the sky told him he should have time before it reached Harmony Creek to hurry to the Hartz farm and put Slim in their barn.

Eli was about to turn the buggy around when a county sheriff's car sped past in a blur. It was followed moments later by a state police vehicle.

The pager at his waist buzzed.

Looking at the code, he saw it was a request for all available firefighters to rush to the firehouse. Was there a fire in Salem? Or was it in a nearby town, which meant sending Salem's firefighters and equipment to work with the local department to put out a major fire?

"Go," he shouted to Slim as he slapped the reins on the horse's back.

Startled, Slim broke into a near run.

Eli pulled Slim to the right as more emergency vehicles—both state police vehicles—zipped past. The buggy rocked. Not from the cars speeding by, but from a gust coming out of the storm. Thunder cracked nearby. He ignored the storm as he raced the buggy toward town and the firehouse.

He hoped he'd be in time.

Chapter Sixteen

When Eli reached the intersection in the heart of the village, he was shocked to see traffic being rerouted along West Broadway toward the post office. Nobody—not even pedestrians—were being allowed to go north on Main Street.

He glanced at the sky, but saw no dark smoke to indicate that there was a fire. What was going on?

As he reached the intersection, a man in a sheriff's uniform held up his hand. "You can't go through."

"I'm a volunteer firefighter, and we've been called in."

The deputy sheriff motioned to another man. The older man wore a state police uniform. He asked what the problem was. He barely glanced in the buggy's direction, keeping his attention on the deputy.

"Let him through," said the state policeman and walked to where he'd been standing by a length of yellow tape that crossed the street from one corner to the other. He didn't pay attention to the lightning and thunder that were getting closer by the second.

"Stay as far left as you can at the intersection," the

deputy said. "We need to keep the intersection clear for emergency vehicles to come through."

"What's going on?"

"A robbery."

He must have misread the officer's lips. "What did you say?"

"A robbery." He hooked a thumb toward the northern end of Main Street. "Someone is robbing the hardware store."

Hardware store? Mercy had said Miriam was taking Kyle to the hardware store.

He scanned the street. He didn't see Kyle's bright red hair or a white *kapp*. Where were they?

Pulling his buggy beside the library across the street, he lashed Slim's reins to a planter. He glanced up the street at the array of police cars, with lights flashing. Nobody was going to let him through there.

The alley by the hardware store! Could he sneak in that way? He jogged toward the rear of the soda shop on the corner. Looking between it and the tiny antiques store next door as lightning danced in the sky overhead, he frowned. The way was blocked by several high fences, plank and chain-link. He kept going away from Main Street. Past the stone church was an open lot with a large stone to mark where a fort had stood during the Revolutionary War.

He almost let out a cheer when he saw a clear path to the alley between the hardware store and the diner. He squinted through the dim light, but saw nobody there. Forms moved stealthily on the far side of the hardware store. If he could slip past them, he would come out on Main Street.

*Keep Miriam and Kyle in Your hand, Lord, and if it's
Your will, let me get to where I can help them.*

Using the plank fences to shield him from any eyes,
Eli slipped into the alley. Sounds were distorted by the
close walls, but he guessed someone was using a bull-
horn to communicate with the thieves.

He stepped out of the alley, sidling to his left to blend
in with the handful of people standing on the diner steps
and watching the police officers. Eli listened as a man
related in a frightened voice how he'd escaped out the
door seconds after the robbers entered.

"Anyone else in there?" Eli asked.

"Yep. Tuck is." The man gulped. "And I saw a
woman and a kid."

The world seemed to tilt, and Eli grasped the iron rail
by the steps. Could that be Miriam and Kyle?

"Do you know who they are?" someone else asked
before he could.

The man nodded, his eyes wide with terror. "They
must be one of those Amish families that have moved
into the hollow by Harmony Creek. The woman had on
a thin white thing on her head. Like those women wear."

Eli dropped to the step. Eyes riveted on him and his
plain clothing. He saw mouths moving and concerned
expressions, but he couldn't take in a single word. He'd
never understood what it meant not to be able to catch
his breath…until now.

"Don't do anything stupid," the taller man with the
black ski mask said as he waved a gun between Tuck,
who was behind the counter, and Miriam and Kyle,
who still stood by the tool wall. "Give us the money,
and we'll go. Nobody gets hurt."

"All right, all right." Tuck raised his hands over his head as he edged toward the register.

"Listen to them," Miriam whispered to Kyle, whom she kept behind her.

The shorter man growled something in their direction, and Miriam clamped her lips closed.

When the bell on the cash register rang, the sound echoed through the silent store. It was followed immediately by the scream of a siren coming along the street. Tires squealed as one vehicle, then another, came to an abrupt stop in front of the hardware store.

The two thieves exchanged an anxious look at the same time Miriam and the man behind the counter did. Would the thieves realize the futility of continuing or would the arrival of police make them more desperate?

She must make sure the little boy obeyed. "Kyle?"

No answer.

"Kyle?" she whispered, a bit louder as she prayed her voice would be lost in the screech of more sirens.

Again, she got no answer.

Risking a glance over her shoulder, she saw no sign of the little boy. Her heart exploded into her throat. Where was he? How could she protect him if she didn't know where he was? No matter what Eli thought, she held tightly to her vow to keep Kyle safe.

She couldn't draw attention to herself. Without moving, she scanned the sections of the store she could see. A door at the back was ajar. Had it been that way before? Maybe Kyle had seen his chance to escape and had taken it. She hoped so.

As the two men debated, she heard a soft rattle near the open door. Kyle? Why hadn't he fled? There must be an exterior door for deliveries. Was it locked? She didn't dare to keep looking, not wanting the men to notice her interest in the half-open door.

Suddenly, the two men came along the counter and ran toward the back door. She took a step to follow, but was shoved aside. She hit the floor hard and stared in horror as the men rounded the counter.

With a shout, the shorter man collided with the other thief.

"Watch out!" the man in the black ski mask shouted.

The shorter man growled a curse and shoved his fellow thief. "You watch out. Don't run into me."

"I didn't. You bumped into me. Let's get out—" He screeched as he lost his balance on marbles strewn across the floor.

Kyle's marbles?

Miriam held her breath as the thief's shoulder hit a display of keys, knocking it off the shelf. Blank keys flew in every direction. She took the opportunity the chaos provided to look toward the door that was ajar. She saw Kyle peeking out around it. She motioned him to hide.

Too late.

The shorter man caught Kyle by the sleeve and dragged him into the store.

"I'll show you what happens to little boys who get involved in something that's not their business." He raised his gun toward the *kind*.

Kyle's grin vanished along with every bit of color in his face. Tears flooded his eyes that locked with Miriam's.

She didn't stop to think. She jumped to her feet and between Kyle and the gun. Shouts came from everywhere as she shoved Kyle behind a stack of paint cans.

At the click of the trigger, she prayed the bullet wouldn't hit her or the boy.

Protect him, Lord! Eli needs him.

Everyone in the street froze at the sound they'd prayed they wouldn't hear coming from the hardware store.

A gun firing.

The noise vibrated through Eli's hearing aids and into his heart. The two people he loved most were in that store.

He raced forward as rain began to fall in a torrent. Arms surrounded him like a net, keeping him back. He tried to push them aside. He had to see what was happening in the store.

He had to!

Police ran up the steps, ramming the door open. They carried pistols and long guns.

Eli's gut cramped. Miriam or Kyle could be hit by a ricocheting bullet.

Someone appeared in the doorway. A flash of lightning flickered off white organdy.

Miriam!

Tearing himself away from those trying to hold him back, Eli rushed up the steps. He grabbed her hand and swung Kyle, who stood beside her, into his arms as if he were still a toddler. Racing down the trio of steps, he pushed past the cops heading into the store. He ducked into the alley between the two buildings. He held Miriam against the wall of the diner and stepped between her and the street.

He set Kyle on his feet before looking for any sign of injury on the boy and Miriam. She was clutching the bricks on the wall as if she could drive her fingertips into them. Her face was the color of her *kapp*. She released the wall to put her arm around Kyle as he leaned against her. They stared straight ahead, fear imprinted on their faces.

But he didn't see any blood on them as rain poured down. Had the shot missed them? Had it hit someone else? He'd find out later. For now only the two people in front of him mattered.

"Are you hurt?" he asked.

"We are okay," Miriam said, but her lips trembled so hard he barely could understand what she was saying.

"Are you sure?"

She clasped his face between her hands. "Read my lips, Eli. We—both Kyle and I—are fine."

"But I heard—" He choked on the words.

Kyle tugged on his arm. When he looked at the boy, he was astonished to see his nephew grinning as if he'd just been on the greatest adventure.

"*Onkel* Eli, you should've seen Miriam! The thief aimed his gun at me. She jumped in front of me. Right in front of that guy's gun." His eyes glittered with excitement, and Eli wondered if his nephew was enhancing the tale. "She wasn't scared. Not a bit."

"I was terrified," Miriam said, her voice quavering. "If the taller thief hadn't hit the shorter one's arm and caused the shot to go astray, we might be dead."

"You saved him," Eli said as, in the street, police officers were putting handcuffs on the thieves. He ignored them.

Miriam did, too. "I told you I'd do everything I could to make sure nothing bad happened to him."

"And you did. *Danki*, sweetheart." He tipped her lips beneath his and kissed her so she understood he meant exactly what he was saying.

* * *

By the time the police had hustled the thieves away and interviewed Miriam and Kyle as well as Tuck, the storm had passed. They'd been invited into the diner where the owner put complimentary bowls of hearty soup in front of them. Miriam and Eli sat at a table while Kyle joined Tuck at the counter, who was discussing the merits of the pies on display.

The boy had apologized for erasing the message on the whiteboard at the schoolhouse. He'd wanted to keep his gift a complete surprise.

Miriam put down her spoon after a single bite. "Eli, I need to tell you—"

"I need to tell you…" Eli began at the same time. "Go ahead."

"I need to tell you about what happened before I came to Harmony Creek."

He shook his head. "I know what happened. Caleb told me today."

She lowered her eyes. "You know you were right not to trust Kyle with me."

"Don't." He put a finger to her lips. "Don't say another word about that. Ever. If Yost Fisher couldn't see the obvious fact you saved his son, why do you think he could see anything else? All you did wrong was to believe a man who shifted his guilt onto you." He folded her hand between his as he added, "I'm sorry I did the same."

"I should have told you about all of it before now."

"Just as I should have told you before now about why the wall fell at my brother's farm."

"Which Kyle tells me you believe was your fault,

though it wasn't." She explained what the little boy had told her he overheard.

He didn't reply for several minutes. At last, he said, "I should have listened to Kyle. Just like I should have listened to you, but I refused to believe anyone who told me my brother didn't follow the instructions I gave him for building the wall. I told myself they were trying to make me feel better when I had lost so much."

"I told myself the same thing when others seemed to believe Yost's accusations. People I respected. If they believed it, why shouldn't I?"

"Because we didn't want to think people we loved would think poorly of us. As poorly as we thought of ourselves for failing to be perfect. It's time, my sweet one, to stop worrying about what others think of us and do what we know is right." Raising one hand, he curved it along her cheek. "I asked you to watch over Kyle, and you have. Will you watch over something else for me?"

"What?"

"My heart. *Ich liebe dich.*"

"You love me?" she whispered.

"Ja."

"And *ich liebe dich.*"

"Will you—"

Kyle's voice rose over Eli's. "Oh, no!" cried the boy, jumping off the stool and running to their table.

"What's wrong?" Eli asked.

"I left your gift at the hardware store."

Eli gave Miriam the lazy smile that delighted her. "Don't worry. We'll get it, but first, Miriam, would you give me a gift, too? Would you give me your hand in marriage?"

"*Ja!*" Kyle announced before she could reply. "She'll marry you, and we'll be a real family at last."

She laughed. "I couldn't say it any better than he did. *Ja*, I'll marry you, Eli, and I'm going to stop caring about what others think of me when I know something is right."

"Marrying me?"

"Nobody will doubt that is right." She leaned across the table and kissed him.

When Kyle cheered, the other patrons joined in.

But she heard only the sound of Eli's heart beating with hers, a thrilling melody they'd share for the rest of their lives.

Epilogue

"Miriam, where are you?"

"Coming." She hurried up the stairs of the old farm-house at the far end of the hollow. The house where Eli and Kyle lived. Soon the house would be her home, as well. She stepped into a simple bedroom set close between two dormers and looked through the doorway at the precious people who already had become part of her family.

Eli gave her a warm smile as he took her hand and sat her on the side of Kyle's bed. The little boy was scrubbed, his hair damp from his shower. Cute blue pajamas were bright against his white sheets, but matched one of the colors of his crazy quilt.

"Ready for your story?" she asked.

"Ja." The *kind* wiggled in excited anticipation. "Tell me the story about the day you got chased by the bees."

"You've heard that one a dozen times," Eli said with a laugh.

"But I like the faces Miriam makes when she tells it."

"How about the rest of the chapter in the book we've been reading?" Eli winked at Miriam, and happiness swirled within her heart. "I don't know about you, but I can't wait to hear what happens to the boy and the missing kittens."

"He's going to find them." Kyle rolled his eyes. "You know that, *Onkel* Eli."

"But how? Isn't that the question?"

Miriam leaned forward and patted the little boy's shoulder. "We'll finish the chapter tonight. Remember? Books on school nights and tall tales other nights."

"Okay." Kyle nestled against his pillow. "Are you going to read to us in school tomorrow, Miriam?"

"I plan to." She'd been asked to stay on as the school's teacher for another year. Though it wasn't common for a married woman to teach, she'd continue after she and Eli took their vows. By the time next fall rolled around, she would hand the school over to someone else and focus on making the creaky old farmhouse a comfortable home.

As she read, she kept looking at the man standing in the doorway. He was watching her face. Not to read her lips, he'd told her, but because he enjoyed looking at her and knowing they'd be together for the rest of their days.

She finished the chapter, then listened while Kyle said his prayers. She blinked back happy tears when Kyle asked for a blessing for "*Onkel* Eli and *Aenti* Miriam."

Tucking in the *kind* and giving him a kiss on the forehead, she stepped aside to let Eli do the same. After they'd wished the little boy sweet dreams, she followed Eli down the stairs, which were too narrow for them side by side.

He paused at the bottom and took her hand as they walked out onto the front porch. He didn't release it as they sat together on the swing he'd installed the previous week.

With her head on his shoulder and his arm around hers, they rocked together and gazed at the stars.

"Our wedding plans will be published this Sunday," he murmured against her *kapp.*

She glanced at him. "I know. I can't wait."

"Neither can I." He brushed his lips against hers. "Because I know there's nobody I trust more to keep my heart safe."

He kissed her again, and she knew he could read on her lips how much she loved him, too. It was a message she intended to share with him as often as possible.

* * * * *

If you enjoyed this story,
pick up these other stories from Jo Ann Brown

AMISH HOMECOMING
AN AMISH MATCH
HIS AMISH SWEETHEART
AN AMISH REUNION
A READY-MADE AMISH FAMILY
AN AMISH PROPOSAL

Find more great reads at www.LoveInspired.com

Dear Reader,

Have you ever met a person who was completely happy with his/her appearance or some aspect of their personality? We're all a work in process. Some of us have visible challenges, as Eli does with his hearing aids. Others have invisible ones—for example, Miriam with her lack of self-esteem. Eli and Miriam needed to believe God put these roadblocks in their paths for a reason. They—and we—must accept that by meeting such challenges with perseverance and prayer, each of us becomes stronger in our faith.

Visit me at www.joannbrownbooks.com. Look for my next story coming soon from Harlequin Love Inspired, the next in my series set in Harmony Creek Hollow.

Wishing you many blessings,
Jo Ann Brown

Get 4 FREE REWARDS!

We'll send you 2 FREE Books plus 2 FREE Mystery Gifts.

Love Inspired® books feature contemporary inspirational romances with Christian characters facing the challenges of life and love.

FREE Value Over **$20**

SPECIAL EXCERPT FROM

Love Inspired.

Her family's future in the balance, can Clara Fisher find a way to save her home?

Read on for a sneak preview of
HIS NEW AMISH FAMILY by **Patricia Davids**,
the next book in **THE AMISH BACHELORS** miniseries,
available in July 2018 from Love Inspired.

Paul Bowman leaned forward in his seat to get a good look at the farm as they drove up. Both the barn and the house were painted white and appeared in good condition. He made a quick mental appraisal of the equipment he saw, then jotted down numbers in a small notebook he kept in his pocket.

"What is she doing here?" The anger in his client Ralph's voice shocked Paul.

He followed Ralph's line of sight and spied an Amish woman sitting on a suitcase on the front porch of the house. She wore a simple pale blue dress with an apron of matching material and a black cape thrown back over her shoulders. Her wide-brimmed black traveling bonnet hid her hair. She looked hot, dusty and tired. She held a girl of about three or four on her lap. The child clung tightly to her mother. A boy a few years older leaned against the door behind her holding a large calico cat.

"Who is she?" Paul asked.

"That is my annoying cousin, Clara Fisher." Ralph opened his car door and got out. Paul did the same.

The woman glared at both men. "Why are there padlocks on the doors, Ralph? Eli never locked his home."

"They are there to keep unwanted visitors out. What are you doing here?" Ralph demanded.

"I live here. May I have the keys, please? My children and I are weary."

Ralph's eyebrows snapped together in a fierce frown. "What do you mean you live here?"

"What part did you fail to understand, Ralph? I… live…here," she said slowly.

Ralph's face darkened with anger. Paul had to turn away to keep from laughing.

She might look small, but she was clearly a woman to be reckoned with. She reminded him of an angry mama cat all fluffed up and spitting-mad. He rubbed a hand across his mouth to hide a grin. His movement caught her attention, and she pinned her deep blue gaze on him. "Who are you?"

He stopped smiling. "My name is Paul Bowman. I'm an auctioneer. Mr. Hobson has hired me to get this property ready for sale."

Don't miss
HIS NEW AMISH FAMILY by Patricia Davids,
available July 2018 wherever
Love Inspired® books and ebooks are sold.

www.LoveInspired.com